ADVERSE CONDITIONS

RECLAIMED HEARTS
BOOK 1

ELLE KEATON

ONE

LATE SEPTEMBER

"Abby, it's fine. Jeez, I'm only going a few miles up, to the first lake. It's pack-in pack-out, but there's still usually some good stuff there."

One time he'd found a North Face sleeping bag, in its stuff sack and everything. Probably had fallen off someone's pack. Whoever it had belonged to, they weren't coming back, so Jayden had helped himself to the bag and the other things he'd found over the summer, pawning them in Aberdeen for cash. Every little bit helped.

"It's late, Jay," Abby persisted. "What if it gets dark? If you're not back by dinner, I'm telling Mom."

As if their mother would notice Jayden was gone. She was the reason he'd resorted to rifling through campsites. He wasn't old enough to get a job, and he hated it when there wasn't anything in the house for them to eat. He'd thought about telling a teacher or someone else at school, but what if they made him and Abby go somewhere else, like foster care?

Jayden didn't know anything about how that worked, but he'd heard enough stories about foster care to not want anyone to know he and Abby mostly took care of themselves. Hence

Jayden's new hobby. The backpackers were rich and had nice equipment. If they were foolish enough to leave it behind, they could afford to buy more.

Every single day he missed his dad more, and Abby missed him too. At first it had seemed like an honor to be the man of the house, but the further their mom fell into depression the more he just wanted his dad back home. But his dad's deployment had taken him somewhere so far away this time, they couldn't even talk on the phone.

"I'll be back by dinner, promise." Clenching his fist, he held it out for his sister to bump.

"I wish we had phones," Abby said as she bumped his fist with hers and settled back on the couch with her book of the week. Maybe he'd stop at the library when he went to Aberdeen to sell the stuff.

"Me too, but they don't work around here much anyway. Don't worry."

He couldn't be back too late anyway, he had stupid homework to do. School had only been going for a couple weeks—this year Jayden had started ninth grade, the first year of high school—and it seemed like homework was the teachers' favorite thing. But it was only the end of September, he'd have plenty of time to catch up.

If there was abandoned equipment up at the hike-in sites, it would be ruined by spring or maybe taken by another camp robber. Ruined gear was no good to them. He needed to get up there while the weather held.

Looking both ways, Jayden hurried across the road that ran between Zenith and the forest, then stepped onto the side trail and began walking. This particular trail eventually hooked to the larger one that wound its way up to the lakes. It actually went past the lower lakes to another three or four miles of grueling switchbacks and then to some alpine lakes called the Shepherds' Necklace. Since he'd promised Abby he wouldn't be late, Jayden wasn't planning on hiking that far. He'd be lucky to get home before dark as it was.

On the west side of the forest, past the necklace lakes, the trail turned into Crook's Trail. Most hikers didn't hike it from end to end. They parked on the Cooper Springs side of the woods and hiked up to the lakes to enjoy nature, then turned around and returned to where they'd left their cars, all within a few hours.

As Jayden strode along, the timberland creaked and whistled around him. Tree branches rubbed against each other, and twigs snapped under the soles of his worn-out athletic shoes. Jayden never felt nervous in the woods like Abby did. He liked the whisper of wind and the random chatter of birds as they searched for bugs; he felt a sort of kinship to them. The crows, Steller's jays, eagles, wrens, and warblers all had opinions about him and each other. His favorites were the jays—duh—but he liked them all.

Without heavy gear, and because he used some not-forest-service-approved shortcuts—Critter or Mags would kill him if they ever found out he went off trail—it only took him about an hour and a half to get to the first set of lakes. It was cool how the lakes were invisible until he was about seventy feet from the water. Then, after he rounded a huge moss-covered boulder, there they were, smack dab in front of a person.

The tent area was to his left, so Jayden veered that direction first. If nothing had been left behind in those spots, he'd quickly walk the trail around the lake. Sometimes hikers stayed wherever they wanted even if the signs said not to, and those were usually the ones who lost the best stuff. If he didn't find anything he'd head back home so Abby wouldn't tattle. Fingers crossed he'd find something.

The first site was clean and empty, and Jayden's stomach sank. He'd really hoped to find some stuff up here. At the second site, he scored a Yeti drinking mug sitting by a fire pit. Not much but better than nothing, he supposed. Luckily, they'd made sure the fire was out, but too bad for them they'd left their pricey mug. He tucked it into his backpack.

As he was moving to check out the next site, he abruptly realized the little hairs on the back of his neck were seriously twitching and the higher elevation birds had stopped their chatter. Something was out there. Without being too obvious, he glanced around, trying to see into the woods. Had he been caught? No. Taking this stuff wasn't illegal. Maybe he should take it to the Forest Service offices in Cooper Springs instead of selling it, but hey, finders keepers and all that.

Mountain lions lived in the forest, but he'd thought they mostly stuck to the super rugged parts of the park where the goats lived. Jayden didn't know how to explain it, not even to himself, but whatever was watching him—it felt human, not animal.

He shook his head. He'd listened to too many of Forrest's and Rufus's stories about the Sasquatch who supposedly roamed the woods. There wasn't anyone there. There was no Sasquatch.

If he repeated it enough times, he might believe it.

Instead of hiking around the lake in search of more forgotten belongings, Jayden casually glanced around like he wasn't totally creeped out, then strolled back to the trailhead. As he passed by the boulder, Jayden stepped off the trail into its deep shadow. Maybe if whoever was waiting in the trees thought he was gone, they'd come out of hiding. Even though his instinct was to run, he wanted to know who was there.

A few slow minutes passed, and Jayden started to think he'd imagined the whole creepy feeling when a dark figure shambled out of the woods on the other side of the tent pads and into his line of sight.

What the fuck?

His heart lurched and began pounding against his ribs, a wild bird trying to escape. It was all he could do not to turn and run. Whoever it was stopped too far away for Jayden to see them clearly and he didn't recognize their shape. It wasn't Critter, or Forrest, and for sure not Mags. He knew all of them well enough to recognize their stances from far away.

The figure swiveled and lurched toward the path and the boulder Jayden hid behind. Why had they been watching him instead of just coming out and saying hi? Closer now, he saw that their clothes were worn and their hair stuck up every which way, like a freak out of a horror movie. All they needed was a long shiny cleaver. On second thought, he was glad they hadn't approached him.

Not a Sasquatch. A seriously creepy-looking human man. Not a figment of his imagination and for some reason, that scared him even more.

He'd seen enough. Maybe Abby was right, the forest wasn't safe. Abandoning the protection the boulder provided, Jayden bolted back down the trail for the safety of their shitty house and stupid empty fridge.

Luckily, Jayden could run for miles, especially downhill— being fast helped when he was running from school bullies. But every time he slowed to catch his breath, he thought he heard footsteps on the trail behind him and he sped up again.

Finally, he veered off the main trail to the smaller one and burst out onto the road, legs pumping until he reached the alley that led to their back yard. Vaulting over the gate, he pounded up the back stairs and burst in through the door. Slamming it shut behind him, Jayden collapsed against the door, his heart crashing against his ribs.

TWO
XAVIER

Mid-October

Silver rain beat down on the street outside Xavier Stone's house like the weather gods had been holding it for hours and hours. When the droplets hit the ground, they bounced back up a good two inches. It was fall, but it was still early for such a nasty storm.

Xavier was talking on the phone with his cousin as he observed the deluge from the comfort of his living room, hoping there'd be a break in the downpour soon. Whether he liked it or not, he *was* going to have to head outside. But for the time being he was doing what any self-respecting Pacific Northwest native did in a situation like this one—staying inside with his raincoat on, prepared to race out the door at the first sign of the storm letting up.

"You've got this in the bag, Xav," his cousin Daisy assured him for the nth time.

He glared at the liquid continuing to gush from the low dark clouds squatting over Cooper Springs, continuing to add to the mini rivers that ran down the road in front of his house and into the swales, ditches, and storm drains meant to control it.

Squinting, Xavier moved even closer to the window so he could see down to the end of the street.

"Dammit."

"What?"

"There's a puddle the size of a small lake at the end of the block."

Fall leaves must be clogging the storm drain again. Unless he, Xavier Stone, dragged his butt out there and removed them, the whole street would flood. But if he did that, he'd be taking his Brooks Brothers suit in to be cleaned and pressed again. Good dry cleaners were hard to find in this corner of the state.

"That's nothing. The Tainted Crown's entire parking lot flooded a couple days ago."

Crap weather wasn't a surprise for this time of year, especially in the shadow of the Olympic Mountain range. Cooper Springs was on the western edge of the Olympic Peninsula in Washington State, the first point of contact for storms rolling off the majestic Pacific Ocean. Any further west and the town address would actually be *in* the ocean. The surprise was that Xavier had returned to soggy Cooper Springs after moving away as a young man.

It seemed Cooper Springs was in his blood, even after spending two decades denying it. Ten months of rain, two months of intermittent sunshine, and—Xavier glanced across the street to Liam Wright's fisherman's cottage and his cluttered front yard—an infinite amount of chainsaw art.

"Why did I buy here again?" Xavier muttered into the handset. He had a landline because this was the Olympic Peninsula, and residents here knew not to rely on cell phones. Another fun quirk of the area.

"Because you love your hometown. And you want to be close to your favorite cousin but not close enough so I can drop in unexpectedly," replied Daisy. "That's me. I'm your favorite cousin, in case you've forgotten."

"You're my only cousin," Xavier pointed out.

"What can I say? I'm not lucky enough to have an identical twin. Can you even imagine two of me? World domination! Speaking of, have you decided to forgive Max for being human?"

Xavier snorted. Not really, but he'd get over Max's stupidity. Or Max would come to his senses. He and Maximillian hadn't talked much since the DNA testing had—unfortunately—revealed their bio-dad had another family. One he'd deserted for Max and Xavier's mother, Wanda. Their mom hadn't known either, although they all had known Dad was a tool.

Max wanted to make things right with the Other Family. Xavier figured they wouldn't want to have anything to do with sons born while the tool was still married to their mother. Mom was still reeling from the news and claimed she did not have an opinion. She refused to discuss it with Xavier or Max. At the moment, there was a detente on further rehashing of the past—and Xavier was fine with that.

"If you had more cousins, I'd still be your favorite," Daisy stated with irritating smugness. "You don't have to butter me up. I'm confident in my status as Most Favored Cousin."

She was, and Xavier knew it.

"I don't suppose you want to buy some real estate around here?"

More of Daisy's infectious laughter flowed across their connection.

"I have enough trouble finding clients up here! Rexville isn't exactly the center of the universe. And there's the pesky new land management committee demanding all my time."

"At least you don't have Rufus Ferguson claiming he spotted a Sasquatch in the woods behind town. I'm pretty sure all Chief Dear spent the first half of the month doing was responding to calls claiming 'suspicious hairy guys' had been spotted on the outskirts of town." This was Cooper Springs—about half the male population was hairy and could use a shower.

Daisy laughed again. It buoyed Xavier to know his cousin totally understood what he was dealing with in Cooper Springs.

"What's going on down there anyway?" Daisy asked, thoughtfully. "This isn't the first time you've told me about something like this."

Xavier sighed. "You know how it is here. Somebody is always seeing something." Or nobody saw anything. He scraped his fingers through his hair. "Maybe Rufus *is* onto something. Not Bigfoot, of course, but something weird. We've had people breaking into empty homes, and forest rangers had to remove an encampment a few weeks ago. Critter said it was well-hidden and had been there a while. The *residents* had not been thrilled to be hurried along."

Mike Zweig, better known as Critter, was the senior forest ranger. He'd run the tiny log-cabin-styled Forest Service office at the edge of Cooper Springs for more than a decade. A staunch protector of the forest and wildlife in their region, he took his job very seriously.

"Little town with big-city issues. I get that."

Xavier had only moved back last spring. Cooper Springs was his hometown, but he was still refamiliarizing himself with its heartbeat. Things had changed in the years he'd been gone but—except for a rise in break-ins and Sasquatch sightings —the change was positive.

"If my half-baked plan is at all successful, maybe Cooper Springs will be better equipped to deal with future big-city crises. It's not as if hunger and homelessness are magically going to go away."

Rexville was small too, like Cooper Springs, but at least the town had Daisy Stone in its corner. She was single-handedly responsible for the increase in their tax base, having revived a renaissance faire that, even in its first year back, brought in scads of money and tourists who were already booking rooms for next summer. Cooper Springs could definitely benefit from some kind of festival.

He glanced out the window again. Across the street, Liam Wright's most recent chainsaw sculpture was proudly displayed in his front yard. He couldn't quite tell what it was supposed to be; he'd have to ask Liam when he saw him.

"Yeah—" Movement in the yard next to Liam's caught Xav's attention. He leaned closer to the windowpane for a better view of his hunky, muscly neighbor as he stomped out into the street. The man carried a long-handled yard tool slung over his shoulder like some character out of a Monty Python movie and was dragging a clean green bin behind him.

Halting at the corner, he hefted the cast iron grating off in one swift movement and began aggressively raking the leaves and other debris out of and away from the drain. Even though he was bundled up in a yellow rain slicker, Xavier would have recognized the Samaritan anywhere. "And also, you don't have to deal with Vincent Barone."

Vincent Barone. *His nemesis.*

All Xavier wanted to do was sell property and help Cooper Springs grow. But Vincent Barone had decided to get himself certified as a real estate appraiser and stymie Xavier at every fucking turn. Every damn *i* and every damn *t* that possibly needed dotting or crossing—and many that didn't—were mentioned in every single one of Barone's reports. Didn't Barone understand that there needed to be room for negotiation? Maybe Mrs. Nelson's estate didn't want to fix the roof and would instead reduce the sale price for a potential buyer.

"It's his literal job, Xavier," Daisy reminded him with a laugh. Probably hoping to stop the rant she'd spotted from over a hundred miles away. "He is supposed to find things the seller should fix. No one wants the surprise of the AC failing the day after move-in."

"He won't listen to reason, Daisy," Xavier grumbled. "He is literally the most aggravating person in all of Cooper Springs. There's a guy coming all the way from Seattle *today* to look at the cabins and I know Vinny-boy is going to screw it up—if it gets as far as an offer."

Barone *was* extremely thorough. Which was great when building bridges or, in Vincent's case, teaching shop at the high school and needing to make sure the bored teenagers didn't cut their extremities off. But Vincent's *part-time* second job was home appraisal, and Xavier was tired of being surprised by what Barone wrote up in his official reports. At least give a guy a heads-up that the sump pump had backed up into the garage and caused water damage. Even if Barone had noted that the damage "appeared to be years old," banks hated comments like that. Banks wanted to hear about new roofs and perfect sewer lines, not repairs that could reduce the value of their investment. And Xavier liked to be prepared with the bad news before he talked to his clients, not in the middle of meeting with them.

How fucking hard was that?

"Have you actually tried talking to him? Or do you just stand at your window and shoot dagger glares through the plate glass?"

Xavier moved away from the window so he wouldn't be lying when he said, "No."

"No, what? You haven't talked to him? Or you've quit lurking and eyeing him through the curtains?"

Damn Daisy for visiting last summer and catching Xavier watching Vincent unload his truck after a trip to the local lumberyard. It was a good thing she didn't know about their high school feud. He still hated Vincent with the passion of one thousand burning suns, but he wasn't opposed to the eye candy. It made up for the constant aggravation.

"Did you hear me say someone is coming out to look at the cabins?" Xavier asked to distract Daisy.

"The old resort?"

"Yep." Xavier had a good feeling about this potential buyer. Martin Purdy had the cash and was excited for a change from city to country life. The cabins had, more or less, been on the market for years, just waiting for the right person to come along. Unfortunately, during those years, they'd fallen further and further into disrepair. What had once been a thriving business that brought families and couples to town was now a bit of an eyesore.

A lot of an eyesore.

"Hopefully, this guy, Martin Purdy, has deep pockets and an overwhelming desire to do a lot of remodeling."

"They're still livable, right?"

Xavier considered the once-cute little cabins with their now peeling paint, rotten window sashes, and, in one case, blue tarp covering the roof as extra insurance against the weather. He wondered if the tarp was holding against the weather today.

"Mostly." He tried to make the word not sound like a question.

Xavier watched as Barone tossed the last of the mucky, rotting leaves into the clean green bin, saving the neighborhood from flooding—today anyway. Xavier continued to watch as he strode back across the street to his house, slightly kitty-corner from Xavier's. It was impossible not to notice how Barone filled out his rain pants and yellow slicker like the damn things were tailored for him. Who looked good in those? Apparently, Vincent Barone did.

Xavier sighed. It was a shame Vincent was an uptight jackass—and also most likely straight, seeing as he had a teenaged daughter—because Xavier wouldn't have minded helping him strip out of his wet gear.

"Are you even listening to me?"

"Uh..." Xavier shook his head. "Sorry, what were you saying?"

"Oh, Xav, what am I going to do with you? Has the hunk of man gone back inside now?"

Xavier saw his neighbor's front door close but didn't deign to reply to Daisy's question. And besides, the rain had let up a bit.

"Ha, ha, ha. Look, I need to get going. I'm meeting the guy from Seattle in just a few minutes."

"Good luck!"

A midnight-blue SUV Xavier didn't recognize was parked in the lot of the real estate office when he arrived.

"Sorry." The man waggled his cell phone at Xavier as he wove around the puddles to stand next to him under the cover of the eaves. "I would have called to let you know I'd arrived, but I don't have any service."

Martin Purdy was a good-looking man, possibly a few years older than Xavier. He had that outdoorsy look so many Pacific Northwest natives had, like he'd be just as comfortable climbing a mountain as hanging out in a coffee shop. A dark knit cap covered most of his hair but what Xavier could see of it was shot with silver—much like Xavier's.

Martin looked like the geology professor Xavier knew he'd been until recently. Maybe a bit pale, but it was fall and Xavier doubted even people like him went hunting for rocks in this weather.

"Full disclosure," Xavier replied as he pushed the door open, flipped on the lights, and motioned for Purdy to pass by him into the office, "cell service isn't exactly reliable around here. Definitely invest in a landline, you will need one."

"What about internet?" Martin asked. "Everybody wants that these days."

"Wi-Fi isn't an issue at the resort, and there's a landline already in the office. It's just the cell service that can get sketchy."

Thank god, otherwise he'd be both out of business and have no way to stream his favorite shows. Some of which were definitely of the adult variety.

"Oh, I forgot to officially introduce myself." The man stuck his hand toward Xavier. "Martin Purdy, nice to meet you."

Martin's grip was firm. "Xavier Stone, call me Xavier. Have a seat." He gestured to the client chair adjacent to his desk. "We can go over a few things, then head over to the cabins. You can follow me there, or we can drive together."

As Xavier was setting his parking brake, Cooper Springs' finest sped by with their lights flashing but no siren. Hopefully, it was nothing major and not another Sasquatch sighting. Since late summer, rumors had been flying around town, even more than usual. Rufus Ferguson was even talking about setting up a hotline for sighters to call in to. Frankly, Xavier didn't think people who thought they'd seen a mythical beast needed *more* encouragement.

Climbing out of his BMW SUV, he surveyed the resort, doing his best to see it through a buyer's eyes. The cabins had been built on a rise on the west side of town with a one-hundred-and-eighty-degree view of the Pacific Ocean. These days a builder wouldn't be allowed to develop the bluff, but in the mid-twentieth century, when the resort was built, the coastline hadn't been protected the way it was now.

There wasn't much remotely resort-like about the tract any longer. The property itself was comprised of twelve small cabins built in the 1950s, when Americans were living the dream and traveling the newly built highways like 101 for fun and adventure. The second wave of exploration, as Xavier's grandfather had liked to call it.

Martin had decided to drive himself, the gravel crunching under his tires as he pulled his SUV in next to Xavier's car. Opening the door, Martin stepped out and barely missed a puddle just inches from his front tire. The rain had stopped for the moment, but surely the man should be used to it since he was from Seattle.

"Well," Xavier said, "er, here it is." Inwardly, he cringed. He was supposed to be trying to sell the place, not chase buyers away. "The buildings need a lot of TLC," he added lamely. As if the man couldn't see for himself.

Breathe. Channel your inner Daisy, he told himself.

The cabins were run-down, there was no getting around it. Even from the parking lot where he and Martin stood, it was easy to see the need for repairs. The roofs were encased in vibrant green moss and many of the windows were cracked—missing entire panes in a few cases—and that one roof was still covered with a tarp. But it was all about the potential. The main house nearest the road and at the bottom of the rise—if the structure could be called that—still looked pretty good. There was also a covered shellfish cleaning station and a few picnic tables. Admittedly, they were probably splinter farms. But there was that view.

The last owner, old Mr. Davies, had lived in the lower building and kept up the cabins as best he could until his grandchildren convinced him he'd be happier somewhere else. Xavier didn't know if Davies had been happier elsewhere, but he *did* know he'd passed away less than a year later.

"Can I walk around?" Martin asked.

"Of course," Xavier replied, glad the rain had stopped for now. "That's what we're here for. We can even go inside."

Together they made their way across the gravel parking area.

"When was the last time the cabins were rented out?"

Xavier had sort of wanted to avoid this question, even though the answer was in the disclosure documents. He'd hoped not to have to deal with it quite so soon. "As vacation rentals? It's been a few years—at least ten, I believe."

Purdy frowned. "Was it used for something else? Like, something bad—meth or something?"

Xavier couldn't blame Purdy for his guess. Meth was big in

the region. Cooper Springs had lost more than their fair share of their population to the insidious drug.

"Oh, no. Nothing like meth. But…" He might as well spit it out. "The estate has leased out one of the cabins. The occupant acts as security in exchange for payment, keeps his eye out, makes sure vandals don't break in and the like. Cooper Springs is cute, not perfect."

They'd made it up the wide drive to the line of cabins facing the ocean. His client took in the small structures, the weeds, the cracked blacktop, the general air of abandonment. Inside his coat pocket, Xavier crossed his fingers. *Please, please, please.*

"This is beautiful." Martin breathed out the statement with reverence, spinning around in a circle to take in everything he could see.

Yes. Xavier did a mental fist pump.

Almost the moment the words left Martin's lips, the door to cabin five opened and Xavier's other nemesis stepped outside. At least Vincent showered on a regular basis.

"Morning, Nick," Xavier offered with a smile and pointed stare. "Just showing the property."

"You didn't bother to call, did you?" Nick said, scowling.

Could the man *not* always look like he'd been rode hard and put away wet? Nick's washed-out Levi's were one thread away from falling off his hips and the hoodie he wore needed a good laundering. The man himself needed a good laundering.

"I did, and you didn't answer, so I left a message." To Martin, Xavier said, "Martin, this is Nicolas Waugh. He's leasing cabin five for a few months."

"For a few months," Nick scoffed. "Until the end of next year, you mean. It's in the lease."

Surely Martin Purdy had read the online disclosure statement that mentioned there was a tenant. Xavier took another good look at Nick and sighed. He really needed a shower and a haircut.

Was it impossible for him to take care of himself? The man needed a keeper.

Nick was in his early thirties, Xavier thought, and had returned from South Asia—Indonesia? Or maybe Sri Lanka— six months ago, underweight and grumpy as hell. Also jobless, which was why the Davies estate had hired him to look after the place. Break-ins and vandalism had already driven down the value of the property.

Next to Xavier, Martin stirred and stepped toward Nick, smiling with his hand outstretched. "Good morning, Nick. Martin Purdy, great to meet you. Soon, with any luck at all, I'll be the new owner of Cooper Springs Resort!"

Nick's already hostile expression hardened further as he eyed Martin, one side of his mouth curling upward. He glared at Martin and then down at Martin's hand. "Still nothing good about the morning." Turning, he stepped back into the cabin and slammed the door behind him.

"Well," Xavier said cheerily, "*that* went better than expected."

THREE
VINCENT

"*Please*, Vincent, try not to go overboard on this one," Sydney Baskin implored. "The buyer is planning on paying mostly cash. Only a small percentage of the sale price is financed, just so he'll have cash for improvements. I'm not asking you to fudge details, but this is an important sale for the community."

Vincent's nostrils flared in irritation. "If *overboard* is what you think making absolutely sure I miss nothing and do my job to the best of my ability, then maybe you hired the wrong person."

He was fully aware that Cooper Springs, as a town, was on life support, but he had an obligation to purchasers.

The phone line went silent again. Shit. Maybe he *was* close to getting fired.

"You're not letting me go, are you?" He couldn't even say the word fired. Romy needed braces and then there were the fees for drama club and fuck all what else a teenaged girl required. Every time he turned around, it seemed like there was some new fee, and they added up fast. Whoever said kids were cheap was one hundred percent not living in the twenty-first century. Or didn't have kids. Maybe both.

"No, we're not letting you go. But you can't afford any more complaints."

Scowling, Vincent whirled around to stare out his window toward his archenemy's house. *Xavier Stone.* That entitled jackwagon had been complaining about him. Vincent was sure of it. And his bitching was going to cost Vincent his job.

A fat rain drop smacked against the picture window. Big surprise, it was raining again, as it had been all damn week.

"Vincent," Sydney said warningly.

"What?" he spat, turning away from his view of the 1890s three-story gingerbread Victorian that Xavier Stone had purchased when he moved back to Cooper Springs. The house was pink. Pink! Vincent hated it. The house was the very definition of gaudy and tasteless. And why did a single man need all that space? He and Romy did just fine in their less-than-eight-hundred-square-foot rental. *Just fine.*

"Look, there've been some complaints about your reports. From both buyers and sellers who want to, well, buy and sell. I need you to run your summary past Thomas or me before you turn it in this time."

Vincent sighed heavily. How lovely to be treated like a kindergartner. "Fine. What's the address?"

"You won't need one. It's for the Cooper Springs Resort. Can you have it done by the end of next week?"

After agreeing that, yes, he could have the report done in that time frame, Vincent clicked off and set the phone down on the side table. He could do this. For the sake of Romy, he would play nice and look the other way—unless it was life-threatening, of course, but that went without saying.

The entire town as well as the owners of the falling-down resort would welcome a buyer who would be willing to fix it up and bring tourists back. Any resident in Cooper Springs over the age of forty had fond memories from when the resort was still in full swing, drawing visitors who came for the wide-open beaches, saltwater taffy, crab feeds, and the kite festival. Could tourists be lured back?

When the timber mill had shut down forever in the eighties, residents had started moving away, taking their tax dollars with them. Compounding that, the town leaders had made a series of terrible decisions. Not allowing a community college satellite campus to move into town. Denying permits for a large grocery store. Why stay in a town when the closest groceries were a forty-minute drive away? And now they were talking about cutting funding to the community transit system.

Maybe if the resort opened again, some of the things Cooper Springs had lost would return and a new generation of tourists would help spread the word.

Except for saltwater taffy. Vincent hated that stuff.

Movement on the street caught his attention. It wasn't his daughter Romy, she was already home, in her bedroom, doing whatever scary thing teenaged girls did—plotting their inevitable takeover of the patriarchy or something.

His shoulders hunched against the misty rain, Xavier Stone strode purposefully down the other side of the street, heading toward his house. Where was his fancy BMW? It definitely wasn't a day for a stroll, seeing as the rain hadn't let up since morning. Maybe he'd left it for an oil change. Silas Murphy's auto shop was only a couple blocks away.

Shaking his head, Vincent reminded himself that he was pissed off at the real estate agent for trying to get him fired. Before he thought better of it, he flung his door open, stomped down the concrete steps, and started yelling Stone's name. Rain be damned, they were having this conversation right now.

Xavier stopped walking and slowly turned his head, looking over his shoulder at Vincent.

"What?"

The single word dripped with exasperation. Well, screw him. Stone could fucking be exasperated for the rest of his life.

"Quit trying to get me fired for doing my job correctly."

Vincent figured Stone knew exactly which job he was referring to.

Unnamed emotion flitted across Stone's face. Frustration? Anger? *Is this guy batshitcrazy?* Vincent wasn't entirely sure which. Maybe all three.

Spinning around, Stone stepped off the curb, narrowly missing a puddle the size of Crescent Lake, and stormed across the street toward Vincent. Vincent braced himself. He hadn't expected this reaction. Not from Xavier Stone, who never let anything get to him. He was impervious.

Xavier charged up the walk, close enough that Vincent saw the fierce light in Stone's golden-brown eyes. It was impossible to ignore. "What about you don't mess with me, Vincent Barone? What about you do your job and I'll do mine? People in Cooper Springs are depending on me"—he thumped a fist against his chest—"to sell property, help the community grow, and every time you're the appraiser, there's some inane hoop for us to jump through. *The beauty bark is too close to the foundation...* are you fucking kidding me?"

"The bark was too close," Vincent protested hotly. "It can cause rot and flooding."

Stone narrowed his eyes further. "You *still* think you can play god, huh? *Still* deciding what's right for people, aren't you? News flash, it's not going to make you any friends."

"I have plenty of friends," Vincent shot back. "I don't need some flashy real estate maven wannabe who crawled back to town after failing in the big city to be my friend. I just need to do my job without you interfering." Vincent barely stopped himself from jutting his chin out. He hated how Stone got under his skin just by looking at him.

"Flashy wannabe?" The amber of Stone's eyes was molten now. Vincent stepped back. "At least I left Cooper Springs and made something of myself instead of wallowing here, teaching high school shop and passing judgment on people. Or getting married and divorced."

Stone's angry glare changed to chagrin and was directed behind Vincent over his shoulder. Vincent turned to see his daughter standing in the doorway.

"Dad? Are you okay? What's going on?"

At fifteen, Romy was a sophomore in high school and both the light of Vincent's life and the bane of his existence. When he'd been fifteen, he hadn't been nearly as worldly as Romy. She was smart, pretty, ambitious, and Vincent would lay down his life for her. If she didn't inadvertently kill him first.

"Nothing, just having a conversation with our neighbor." Vincent gestured behind him.

"Pretty loud conversation you guys were having." Romy did not look impressed. Before taking off for parts unknown—thank the gods for that miracle—Carly had always complained she'd birthed a mini Vincent. What could Vincent say to that? It wasn't as if he'd been in charge of the DNA distribution. "If you're done sharing your life with the entire neighborhood," she said, her tone dripping with sarcasm, "the timer beeped."

Right, there was leftover lasagna in the oven.

"I'm coming."

Leaving his troublesome neighbor behind, Vincent made his way back into the house. He'd started to shut the door when he heard Stone's voice. "For the record, I haven't complained about you, but you can bet your ass I'll be making a phone call tomorrow."

Vincent ground his molars together as he forced himself not to respond. He'd done enough damage already.

. . .

Romy was already back in the kitchen, sitting at their small table. She looked up when he entered the room but said nothing, only raising one dark eyebrow, a skill she'd definitely gotten from her mother. Vincent figured he had maybe a minute before he was on the receiving end of a lecture. Even the pre-lecture thirty seconds of complete quiet was the same as Carly's had been.

Sliding an oven mitt over one hand, he turned off the timer and opened the oven door. Heat flowed out, steaming his glasses. He waited a second for them to clear up before pulling out the hot baking dish and setting it on the top of the stove. *Three, two, one...*

"Seriously, Dad, what is your problem? Mr. Stone is perfectly nice. Last week when I was hanging out with Violet and Char at Pizza Mart, he offered us rides."

Vincent blanched and stared at his daughter in disbelief. "You *did not* get in a car with a stranger." The anger that had started to fade returned full force. He flung the oven mitt on the counter and grabbed plates and a spatula, all the while loudly sucking oxygen in through his nose.

"*Dad,*" Romy said with an exasperated sigh as she got up and dug in the silverware drawer for forks. "Mr. Stone is not a stranger. He is our neighbor and everybody in town knows him. He asked right in front of Janelle Wright and Maria Flores. If I had gotten in the car with him and something happened, they would've known where I was. But I didn't because I knew you'd flip your lid. Instead, I walked home. *In the rain.*" She smacked a fork down at each of their spots and sat back down.

Clearly, Romy still wasn't happy about the walk in the rain. Too bad. He was proud of her for making the right choice.

"You bet I'd flip my lid. You are my daughter, and you know better."

They'd had this conversation at least a hundred times. As a girl, she needed to be extra careful. There were creeps everywhere. Last summer, a girl had gone missing from Aberdeen. Vincent hated seeing the missing-person posters tacked to telephone poles and walls all over town. It was so many levels of wrong. People purposefully hurting other people upset him.

Was it fair that the vulnerable had to look out for themselves? No, but Romy following his rules meant—hopefully—he wouldn't be one of those parents wondering when the police would knock on his door. He had a hard enough time giving her the freedom he knew she needed now. The half-empty jug of antacids in the bathroom cabinet was evidence of his constant worry. Angrily, he dug into the pasta, plopping a serving on each of their plates before setting them on the table.

"What's up with you and Mr. Stone, anyway? It's weird how you act around him." She forked a bite into her mouth, chewing as she watched him and waited expectantly for him to just spill his guts.

Yeah, maybe now was not the time to go into the history between him and Xavier Stone.

"Nothing." Xavier Stone rubbed him the wrong way and always had. Always Xavier and never Maximillian, who was Stone's twin. They were identical, but Vincent had always been able to tell them apart. Max never made Vincent see red just by looking at him. Max was an even-keeled good guy. Xavier was baking soda and vinegar.

Romy swallowed her bite and eyed him. "If you weren't my dad and like a million years old, I'd think you had a crush on him. You act like Tiffany Crewe before she and Jason Weaver got together, all pissy and overreacting about stuff. What was that about a complaint?"

The problem with being the single parent of a very smart daughter was that Romy didn't miss much. They'd been Team Barone since Carly'd left them and taken her drug habit along with her. Maybe he needed to be more careful about what he shared with Romy. Were their boundaries too blurred? Vincent worried Romy didn't have a strong female role model, but he was doing the best he could. Except for publicly arguing with his infuriating neighbor.

Who he totally hated and did not have a crush on, and never had.

FOUR

XAVIER

A week or so after the Vincent Barone Incident—and what the hell had *that* been all about?—Xavier was climbing his porch steps when the old-timey ring of his landline reached his ears. He scrambled to get his key into the deadlock before it stopped ringing, but his fingers were cold and stiff and so was the lock.

"Fuck."

By the time he'd wrestled the door open, dashed inside, and fumbled—and dropped—the handset, the caller had hung up.

Glancing at the call screen, he groaned. Why had he bothered to hurry. *Really? Today of all days?*

AH.

Ass Hole.

Also known as Arsen Hollis, aka Xavier's ex.

Arsen lived in Tacoma and Xavier had hoped that the eighty plus miles he'd put between them would deter any further communication. Unfortunately, Arsen couldn't take a hint. He was Teflon-coated, and hints about maybe never seeing Xavier again just dripped off him without leaving a trace.

Peeling off his jacket and tossing across the back of his couch, Xavier considered not returning Arsen's call. But that was like waving a red flag in front of a bull. Arsen would call and call and then he would decide to *drop in for a visit,* regardless of traffic or the eighty-mile drive. Since their breakup was supposed to have been amicable, Xavier would just have to hold his nose and call him back. He would not give Arsen any grist for his rumor mill.

Whatever Xavier had once found attractive in the man had, ages ago, turned to ash. Mr. *T*-crosser *I*-dotter, Vincent Barone, was a far better man than Arsen Hollis. As much as Vincent made Xavier want to pull his hair out, his heart was in the right place. He worked hard, was raising his kid on his own, and was a respected teacher in the community. Arsen plain didn't appear to have a heart and he sure wasn't giving to his community. Every action he took had a value associated with it, like he was an emotional accountant. Too bad it had taken Xavier so long to realize that about him.

All flash and no substance. Arsen gave himself points for everything. Points for giving a dollar to the man standing at the freeway exit ramp—just as the light turned green, so all the drivers behind him witnessed it. Points for reading the popular book club book and talking loudly about it in coffee shops. Points for driving an electric car and crowing about how much he'd paid to save the earth. Points for making sure everyone in his circle knew he sent a check to the senior center each year. And the most points, it seemed, for being nice to his exes, of which there were many, although few of them had actually been friendly—to Arsen. They'd given Xavier looks of understanding, a red flag of epic proportions that Xavier should have heeded.

Reluctantly, Xavier picked up the phone and pressed Return Call.

"Xavier! I was starting to think you were avoiding me!" As always, Arsen sounded jovial, like they were sharing a private joke. It was one thing that had drawn Xavier to Arsen at first. He'd seemed friendly and, even though Tacoma was a more conservative city, didn't hide the fact he was gay, which had been refreshing after a string of still-in-the-closet guys. Xavier later realized that none of it had been about common interest or a mutual attraction. It had been because Xavier fit into the round hole marked "boyfriend" in Arsen's view of himself.

"What's up, Arsen?" Xavier unsuccessfully tried to force cheer into his voice.

"Why so cranky? Is small-town life getting to you?"

Xavier felt his jaw clench. It was as if Arsen had a built-in homing device that zeroed in on whatever was going to most irritate him that day.

"Cooper Springs is fine, Arsen. Lovely, even," he lied since it was the tenth straight day of rain. "Thanks for asking. If that's all you wanted, I'll let you go. I missed lunch and I'm hungry."

"You're not getting off that easily! I'm coming to town. You can show me around and I'll buy us dinner, for old time's sake."

Xavier was immediately suspicious. Why would Arsen be coming to Cooper Springs if not to visit him? He wasn't from town; he had no connections beyond Xavier. There was no Starbucks or five-star restaurant for him to be seen at. He'd have to eat at Pizza Mart with its plywood booths, Formica tables, and jukebox last refreshed in 1988—or worse, the pub. Xavier had zero problem with Pizza Mart or The Steam Donkey. He had fond memories of stuffing himself with pizza when he was a kid, and these days Magnus ordered in the wine Xavier preferred at the pub, but Arsen would *hate* both establishments.

A terrible thought struck him. Where would Arsen be staying? There was literally nowhere in Cooper Springs to stay except for a couple of iffy Airbnbs. *Christ.* Xavier's stomach plummeted.

"Arsen, you can't stay at my house."

"Why not? Is the inn full? I want to see this gorgeous Victorian you left me for and this quaint hometown you decided you needed to move back to."

Xavier forgot to breathe for a moment.

"You just *can't*," he sputtered.

He did his best to drag a calming breath into his lungs. Arsen was a shark and others' anxiety attracted him like blood in the water. Unfortunately, they still had a lot of business connections since Arsen was also in the industry, and real estate was all about networking, even out in Cooper Springs. In fact, networking was how they'd met—because of course it was. Arsen seemed to have dated someone "influential" in most towns between Portland and Bellingham. Which forced Xavier to be polite to Arsen because the man wasn't above spreading rumors. Xavier had no idea how far his reach really was.

He glanced out the window, his mind flailing a little too much like Kermit the Frog did when he had to deal with Miss Piggy. Rain was pelting down and the puddle at the end of the street stretched halfway across the road again. The weather report was full of extreme storm warnings and all the rivers were near flood stage, even the meandering stream the town was named after. If the rain didn't let up soon, parts of town would be under water. Homes might be threatened. His gaze flicked to where Vincent Barone's tiny house sat. Xavier's house was on a rise, but Vincent's? *Not.*

"My neighbor's house flooded," Xavier improvised, trying to sound as if he regretted offering a helping hand to his neighbor. "He and his daughter are staying with me until it gets dried out. It was pretty bad, could take weeks."

Vincent probably wouldn't appreciate Xavier disparaging his house, but a man had to do what a man had to do. Anyway, Vincent deserved it for accusing Xavier of complaining about him. He *had* complained, just not to Vincent's boss.

There was a short silence, during which Xavier could almost hear Arsen thinking.

"That's a shame," he finally said. "Well, I'll be seeing you anyway, as I'm meeting with a client who wants to look at a property out there. Maybe you know it? Cooper Springs Resort?"

That motherfucker. Xavier's blood pressure shot up again. He wasn't fooled by Arsen's innocent tone. Arsen had dug around, researched the property, and now he was going to try and steal Xavier's sale.

Breathe. He could handle Arsen.

Arsen had to know that Xavier and his client, Martin Purdy, were in negotiations with the lawyers for the Davies estate. Xavier had already ordered the appraisal and the inspection. Real estate agents were some of the gossipiest people Xavier knew. The ink wasn't dry on the letter of intent to purchase, but the broker expected the contract by the end of the week. Hell, the letter hadn't even been signed yet.

If Arsen slipped in with a better offer, Martin would be out of luck. And so would Cooper Springs. Xavier seriously doubted Arsen's mysterious client was dedicated to rebuilding the resort the way Martin Purdy seemed to be.

As desperately as he wanted to reach through the phone and throttle Arsen, all Xavier said was, "Let me know if I can answer any questions your client has." He hung up, his heart pounding. Whatever Arsen was up to, he needed to be stopped. He probably didn't have a client, this was just a way to get under his skin. And if Arsen showed up unannounced, Nick Waugh would blow a gasket. That might be fun to watch.

Nick. What was he going to do about him? Xavier appreciated his dedication to protecting the property—there had been several prowlers and none of them were ever caught by the local police. By the time the cops had arrived, whoever it had been, was long gone. There wasn't much left to steal, the cabins had been emptied out years ago, but early last spring someone had broken in and trashed one of the cabins, prompting the estate to hire Nick.

Across the street, Barone's house was still dark. The porch light wasn't on, so his kid wasn't home either. Where was he? Xavier felt the tiniest bit guilty using Vincent as an excuse, but Arsen Hollis was not welcome in his home. Vincent would never have to know about the fake flooding. Arsen would come and go, and Vincent would never be the wiser.

His stomach rumbled, reminding Xavier that he'd missed lunch and it was almost dinner. Changing quickly out of his suit into casual slacks and a button-down shirt, he pulled on his rain gear again and headed back outside. His mom would still be at the shop, and they could have dinner together. At Pizza Mart.

Xavier pushed open the door of the Cooper Springs Thrift Shop and his mom, Wanda Stone, looked up from what she was doing. He shook himself and droplets of water flew off his jacket.

"Young man, can't you read? The Closed sign was turned on."

"Ha, ha. Hi, Mom, love you too."

The neon sign he and Max had bought ages ago for their mom —because the paper one had been so tattered—was glowing red. They'd thought it would add some class to the shop. Wanda had pretended to be offended, but they both knew she'd been secretly pleased.

"Closed doesn't apply to me," he said with his best charming smile.

She graced him with a nearly identical smile in return. Xavier shuffled closer to her, his arms spread wide, threatening her with a very damp hug.

"Don't you think about it." Wanda shook her head at him, grinning as she backed away. "Since you're here, make yourself useful. Take that wet coat off and help me price the rest of this stuff."

Shrugging out of his coat, Xavier draped it over a metal folding chair behind the counter. Wanda handed him a tagging gun and a bag of what looked like baby clothes.

"These are all two ninety-nine."

For a few minutes they worked in companionable silence, just the snick of the guns as they worked. Xavier let the irritation over his phone conversation with Arsen fade away. Wanda had run the thrift shop since Xavier and his twin brother Max were kids, ever since their dad had left their mom for a younger model. At least, that's what his mom had always said. They'd never seen him again, so it wasn't like he could dispute the facts.

The tidy shop was bursting with hand-me-down goods, and the persistent, vague, musty scent of damp and bleach reminded him of how far he'd come. How far both he and Max had come. Max had gone to the Massachusetts Institute of Technology on a full scholarship, joined a software company, and made his first million by the time they were thirty. Xavier hadn't inherited the math gene, but he was happy with his life. Central Washington had been good enough for him. He was good at selling real estate and truly enjoyed helping clients realize their dreams.

It had frustrated both of them that their mom had insisted on staying in Cooper Springs, running the thrift shop like she had since the dawn of time. After years of them offering to buy or build her a house anywhere she wanted, Wanda had put her foot down and said Cooper Springs was her home, *thank you very much.* And in a tone that brooked no argument she'd added, "Someday you two will be thankful I've stayed here."

Finishing up the bag of clothing she'd been tagging and setting her gun down, Wanda broke their companionable silence. "Max called. He'll be here in a little bit."

Xavier paused, not wanting to tag his finger, and frowned at his mom. "What? Not that I don't want to see my brother, but why is he coming down?" They'd just talked a few days ago, and Max hadn't mentioned anything about a visit.

Possibly because Xavier had spent most of the call bitching about Vincent Barone. And *possibly* Xavier had done all the talking in order to prevent Max from broaching the subject of the Other Family.

Max lived in Olympia for the time being. After he'd left the last startup, Xavier had found him a great property in the East

Bay neighborhood. But Max had itchy feet and Xavier didn't expect him to stay there for long.

Wanda shrugged. "He just said he wanted to see us."

Was he sick? Xavier didn't think so. He and Max were identical down to the freckle above their left eyebrow and the way they'd both gone prematurely silver. And they had that woo-woo twin thing people talked about. Even apart, they knew when the other was upset, sick, happy.

Still, he couldn't help asking, "He's not sick or something? Or"—Xavier waggled his eyebrows—"finally met the man of his dreams?"

Wanda shook her head again. "As far as I know, he hasn't met anyone. You two though." She sighed. "I don't need grandkids, but it would be nice to know you're happy before I depart this mortal coil."

"This mortal coil? Have you been in the wine already?" Xavier mocked, pretending to look behind the register. "So much drama. We're both happy, Mom, and you have to admit you didn't like Arsen."

"No, I didn't. I want you happy with the right person." She swatted him with a onesie that had rocket ships and dogs on it. "I'm hungry, let's head to the Mart. I'll leave a note on the door for your brother."

Xavier stared across the table at his brother. "What the actual fuck?" His brother had dropped his version of a nuclear bomb. Maybe that's why he'd been on edge, not because of Arsen, but because of Max. That damn twin connection was a blessing and a curse.

"Language!"

Xavier stared at his mother. "Pardon me, but didn't you teach us those words?"

"Maybe I did. That's not the point."

Pizza Mart was about the usual amount of busy for a rainy midweek evening in October. The familiar scent of pizza dough baking in the brick ovens wafted from the kitchen while *Don't You (Forget About Me)* played over the speakers for what had to be the millionth time since 1985.

A group of girls had taken over a booth and were giggling and laughing. Xavier was pretty sure he recognized Vincent Barone's kid, but he knew better than to embarrass her by saying hello and forcing her to acknowledge his existence. Or maybe he was saving himself. There was something so disturbingly *knowing* about teenaged girls.

"So, yeah, I'm driving out to Jackson, hopefully to meet our older sister," Max repeated as if Xavier hadn't heard him the first time. "We've emailed a couple times since summer. Looks like we have at least one relative in Wyoming who's interested in meeting us—er, me."

"Huh," Xavier said flatly. He had no interest in another sibling or anything else that had to do with their scumbag of a father. The man was dead to Xavier. If he walked into Pizza Mart that minute, Xavier wouldn't acknowledge him.

Max nodded. "Her name is—"

Xavier cut him off with a gesture. "I don't want to know her name. Why are you coming here and telling us this? Do you honestly think Mom wants to have what a wanker Dad was rubbed in her face?"

Max's glance moved from Xavier to their mom, and Xav could see the moment it registered that maybe his mother and brother weren't as excited by his travel plans as he was. As much as they looked alike, Max and Xavier were very different. Until Max'd left for MIT, Xavier had spent a lot of his time keeping an eye out for his nerdy brother because Max had not inherited the cynical gene that protected Xavier, and their mom, from assholes. Their father seemed to be Wanda's only exception. Arsen was an asshole, but Xavier felt like he'd been the result of an error in judgment rather than an overabundance of innocence.

"I'm sorry, Mom, I just..." Max's smile was wobbly.

Smiling, Wanda reached across the table and placed her hand over Max's. "It's fine, hon. I'm not upset you're going, but I'm not really interested in learning about them. Not yet anyway. After all, in this case, *I* was the other woman. Am I right in assuming he"—*he* being their sperm donor, Craig Stone—"was married to her mom too?" She took her hand back and placed it in her lap. Xavier put his arm around her shoulders, offering what comfort he could.

Max nodded, looking back and forth between them. He seemed sheepish now, instead of excited like he'd been when he sat down. "Yeah, he was. I've chatted a couple times with—er, Robin, and yeah, Dad was married. Left when she was a baby."

This was why Xavier was never getting seriously involved with anyone. Sure, he'd like a boyfriend—although, at forty-two, perhaps *boyfriend* was the wrong word—and a better one than Arsen Hollis. But he had rules. No permanent attachments. No empty promises of a future together. *No living together.*

Luckily, since he'd chosen to move back to a zip code with an out-and-proud population still in the single digits, his rules were in no danger of being broken. He and Nick Waugh had less in common than mice and humans. And Forrest Cooper, *interesting* as he may be, was not Xavier's type. At all. Xavier suspected Liam Wright was gay but had never known him to date anyone.

Love would not ambush Xavier Stone in Cooper Springs.

Which, frankly, was a relief. He was tired of dating and all that word entailed, right? Yes, yes, he was.

The bell over the door jingled and Xavier's attention shifted from Max to the man who'd stomped inside. Vincent didn't appear to notice Xavier and his mother and brother tucked away at their corner table. He shook himself much like Xavier had earlier and pushed the hood of his rain jacket off his head before heading directly for the booth of girls. He had to have balls of steel to approach them with such ease.

"Yo, Xav, asshole, pay attention here." Max turned to see who had distracted him. "Hey, isn't that Vincent Barone? The guy who turned you and Forrest Cooper in to Principal Robinson in high school for taking the flag down and running your tighty-whities up the pole? He's your neighbor too, right?"

Xavier grimaced and sighed. That hadn't been one of his finer moments, although at the time it had been hilarious. But Max's prodding reminded him that even twenty-four years ago, Vincent Barone had been a rule follower. So, yeah, he hadn't changed much.

Vincent stood at the end of the girls' booth, radiating impatience. He must be their ride, but the girls were taking their sweet time collecting their stuff. It would have been impossible for Vincent not to feel the extra three pairs of eyes on him. Looking their way, he shot Xav, Max, and Wanda a curt nod before turning back to the girls and telling them to "hustle or they'd be walking to Aberdeen." Seconds later, they were all piling out of the door, leaving the restaurant suddenly much quieter.

Xavier refocused his attention on his mother and brother, only to realize they were both eyeing him with intense curiosity.

"What?"

A slow grin spread across Max's face. "Oh, it's like *that*, is it?"

"Fuck off."

"Language."

"Again, Mom, I learned from you."

"Well, unlearn it."

The door opened again and a thirty-something woman wearing an ill-fitting raincoat and impractical flats blew inside. She had to be freezing. One glance at her expression and Xavier predicted trouble had arrived. She stormed across the tile to the counter and slammed her purse down on it. Wrenching open the bag, she shoved her hand inside it, digging through the contents as she searched for something. For a hot second, Xavier thought she was going for a gun. This was Cooper Springs, after all.

He breathed a sigh of relief when she pulled out her wallet instead.

"How can I help you?" Asked the college-aged employee who'd been in the kitchen.

She stiffened.

"Oh dear," murmured Xavier's mom.

"'How can I help you?'" The woman repeated the poor kid's words back to him in a sing-song voice. "How you can help me is by not making me drive all the way here to pick up your shitty pizza."

And yet here she was, for the shitty pizza. Xavier despised people like her.

"I'm sorry, ma'am, our driver called out sick so we're not delivering to anyone tonight."

"That doesn't help me."

The remaining patrons were all focused on the unfolding drama since it was impossible not to overhear. Besides, town residents lived for drama and now they had a front row seat.

"Um, do you have a pick-up order?"

"Yes, I have a pick-up order." Her voice dripped with sarcasm. "Since I had to drive all the way here from Zenith. It's Harlow."

The clerk stared blankly for a second before realizing that was the order name.

"Who is that?" Max asked Wanda. "I don't recognize her."

"Lizzy Harlow. She's a bit younger than you two. She can be… difficult. She has two kids. Sometimes she stops in the store."

Difficult could mean a lot of things, but in this case, Lizzy Harlow's attitude, her gaunt frame, and that unhealthy skin tone had Xavier thinking it meant drugs.

"Right." The kid typed into the computer. "That'll be thirty-one sixty."

Unzipping her wallet, Lizzy plucked out a card and jabbed it at him. He quickly slid it through the reader. Watching the screen, his eyes widened, and he swallowed nervously. Xavier grimaced. This was not going to end well.

"Um, I'm sorry, ma'am, but this card was declined. Maybe you have another one you want to use?"

"That's not possible, try it again."

He did and the result was the same. By this time another, older employee had emerged from the kitchen, a pizza box in his hands. He'd obviously been listening to what was going on at the counter. Peering over the cashier's shoulder at the computer, he shook his head.

"Maybe it's the weather messing with our system. How about you take the pizza, ma'am, and we'll try your card again in the morning, or even Monday, when the storm has passed."

He held the box out and Lizzy snatched it from him without so much as a thank you. She must have been aware that the entire restaurant had heard the exchange because she spun toward the front door without making eye contact with anyone and pushed back outside.

Wanda sighed. "I think that's what you call a walking disaster."

Max and Xavier both nodded their agreement.

FIVE

VINCENT

"But you aren't a septic inspector," Sydney repeated, her voice sounding tinny over their connection. Obviously, she was finally reading the email he'd sent over the night before.

After hitting Send, Vincent had immediately picked up the phone and called Sydney, but her number had gone to voicemail. He'd left a brief message for her to call him back. He needed Sydney to understand he wasn't being difficult. He was being *thorough*. There was a difference.

"No," Vincent admitted, "I'm not. But the system dates back to the 1980s and should at the very least be modernized. I doubt it will hold up under pressure from a summer of tourists staying there. There could be tree roots growing through it for all we know."

He paced the length of his living room, turned, and paced back in the opposite direction. He'd thought long and hard about including the septic data but in the end, he knew it was the right thing to do. Still, seeing Xavier Stone in Pizza Mart last night had made him feel slightly guilty about it. The man was going to be furious.

"Installing a new septic is a headache. *Oh my god,* just thinking about the permitting is giving me a migraine," Sydney muttered.

Sydney was right. New septic was very expensive these days, especially in a situation with an estuary system like the one that connected their tiny part of the Pacific Ocean to the actual Cooper Springs. He also could've added a bit about future erosion. But the beach was wide, and the cliffs set back far enough that wind, not water, would cause any erosion the buyer had to worry about. A few carefully planted trees would do wonders.

"And what's this about the footbridge?" She asked after another moment. "*Vincent,* we are not including that in the report. It is not part of the physical property. It's just a damn footbridge."

"It's compromised," he said stubbornly, flashing back to the rotten boards and shaky railing.

"The buyer can fix it if they want, that's their decision." Sydney said firmly. "But we're not including it. If the footbridge fails, guests can cut through the marsh like we all did when we were kids. None of us drowned. Christ, Vincent, are you trying to get fired?"

Abruptly, he stopped pacing, his attention focused across the street. A car he didn't recognize stopped in front of Xavier Stone's house, and a man Vincent didn't recognize emerged from the car and stood for a moment, taking the house in. Even Vincent had to admit the house was gorgeous—he didn't really hate it, although the pink was very pink. If he had that kind of money, he might have tried to buy it. But a shop teacher's salary did not lend itself to home ownership.

Xavier's front door jerked open, and the man himself peered out at the visitor with a less-than-welcoming expression on his face. He must have been working from home. The sleeves of his crisp white button-down were rolled up, and he'd unhooked the top few buttons of the shirt so—not that Vincent noticed or anything—a tuft of chest hair peeked out over the third button.

Damn. He repressed the groan that wanted to escape.

Chest hair was his catnip.

Not that Vincent got out much these days with a teenaged daughter at home. But add sexy silver hair and smile lines, all of which his neighbor had in spades, and he was doomed. Luckily for Vincent, Xavier Stone was a jerk.

"Vincent! Are you still there?" Sydney asked, impatience lacing her tone.

"What? Oh, yeah." He sighed. "Fine. I'll take the comments about the septic out."

"Good. And send it back ASAP." She hung up without saying goodbye.

Absently, Vincent set the phone back down and continued watching the drama unfold outside. Xavier had his arms crossed over his chest and his eyebrows were drawn together. Normally, that would make him more irresistible to Vincent. And if that meant he paid too much attention to Xavier's body language, well, Cooper Springs was small, and he was never going to date again anyway. This time though, something about his expression had Vincent wondering if the man was okay. Who was this stranger, anyway?

Without stopping to think deeply about what he was doing, or thinking at all—because he one hundred percent did not like Xavier Stone, even if he was sexy as heck—Vincent shrugged back into his jacket and rain boots, pulled his hood over his head, and stepped outside.

He couldn't help it if he was a neighborly sort.

Vincent knew Xavier had spotted him. It would have been difficult not to, seeing as their houses were almost directly across from each other. As he crossed the street, Vincent thought he read something beyond anger and frustration in Xavier's expression.

Desperation?

"Vincent!" Xavier called out before Vincent opened his mouth to say anything. Or figured out what he was going to say. "Did you get a look at the water damage? Is it still coming inside? I told you that you and Romy could stay here until it was dry. Seriously, it's not an imposition. You need to quit worrying about putting me out."

Vincent did his best to school his expression. Water damage? Staying at Xavier Stone's house? Okaaaay. *Don't look at the stranger, don't wonder what Xavier was thinking.*

"Uh," he mumbled, "it still looks pretty bad. I called that guy in Aberdeen, but he's all booked and can't get out here for a couple more days."

Xavier's head bobbed up and down frantically at his words. "That's terrible, but like I said, my house is your house for as long as you need it."

"Xav, aren't you going to introduce me to your *rugged* friend?" There was a smirk in those words. Why didn't the jerk add *bumbling country hick* too, since he clearly wanted to.

Vincent frowned at the stranger. He was their age, mid-forties, and looked to be wearing a suit underneath his expensive black wool coat. The leather shoes on his feet screamed money and his expression said Vincent did not impress him. But maybe nothing impressed him.

"Vincent, this is," Xavier started, then paused as if he was about to say something else, but instead went with, "Arsen Hollis."

Arsen gave Vincent a dismissive up-and-down glance before returning his attention to Xavier.

Vincent did the same. Two could play that game.

"I was just stopping by as a courtesy," Hollis said to Xavier. "My client and I are meeting at the property in a few minutes."

Vincent noticed a muscle along Xavier's jaw flex as if he was barely controlling himself. What was this stranger doing in town showing real estate? He may drive Vincent crazy, but Xavier Stone was Cooper Springs' agent, not this big-city guy.

He couldn't help asking, "What property?"

"The resort," Xavier ground out.

Vincent opened his mouth and snapped it shut again. Why would this apparent asshole be showing the resort when there was already a contract? His gaze shot back to Xavier. If those weren't begging puppy-dog eyes, he didn't know what was. After all, he had a teenager who used them on him all the time.

"Huh. Uh, somebody is willing to live with Nick for at least a year? When I was—er, driving by yesterday, he had several new sculptures up. Some of them are definitely not PG. And I heard the septic field is on the fritz. No way will anyone get a permit to replace that these days and if they do, it's going to cost them."

Both were true, but Vincent knew they could probably replace parts in the septic system, thus not actually qualifying it as new. No way was he telling that to this asshole. Nick's sculptures? Well, they were just another quirky aspect of Cooper Springs.

Arsen Hollis gave Vincent a second up-and-down look and dismissed him again. Made Vincent want to punch the man. Instead, he tucked his hands in his coat pockets and started toward Xavier's porch. Xavier stepped aside to let Vincent enter his house, offering him a healthy whiff of Xavier's aftershave as he passed by. Something woodsy that reminded him of hiking the trail up to the lakes.

Xavier was saying something to his uninvited guest, but Vincent wasn't listening, too busy taking in Xavier's living room. It wasn't the glam man-cave he'd imagined. He could almost hear Romy accusing him, "Judgey much?" Framed artwork, along with several photographs of Wanda and Max Stone, graced the walls. He stepped closer, wanting to see the pictures in detail.

"Fuck!"

Vincent started and spun around. Xavier was dragging both hands through his hair, making it look like he'd stuck his finger in a light socket. "Thank you for playing along. Arsen infuriates me. I should've known he would show up even though I told him he couldn't stay with me." Xavier's expression shifted from angry to guilty. "I kind of told him your house had flooded, so you were staying with me for the foreseeable future."

The burr of a phone interrupted Xavier's rambling explanation. Vincent patted his pockets, but it wasn't his. Not surprising, since they lived in the deadest dead zone in all of Cooper Springs.

Snatching his vintage-style landline from a table near the window, Xavier put it to his ear. "What?"

Sheesh, even Vincent knew that was no way to answer a call.

"What?" Xavier's gaze shot to Vincent again, eyes narrowed. "You have got to be kidding me. The septic? And the footbridge? No," he muttered as he shook his head, a dark scowl taking over his handsome face, "I'll take care of it."

If looks could kill, Vincent would have been dead and buried five minutes ago. Xavier slammed the phone back down, the sound jarring in the now quiet room.

Wincing, Vincent moved toward the front door. It seemed like he needed to talk to Sydney. Had that been her on the other end of the line? Vincent hadn't submitted the revised report yet. The drama going on outside his window had distracted him.

"What the fuck, Barone? Are you trying to put me out of business? Were you the one who alerted Arsen to the property so he could come and lowball with your shitty appraisal?"

Vincent found himself unable to move, pinned in place by Xavier's icy glare.

"Um..."

"That's all you've got? Um?" Xavier's thick finger poked Vincent's chest. "Do I waltz into the high school and pretend I can teach kids how to run a lathe?" He shook his head. "No, no, I don't. You know why? Because"—his tone dropped to a growl—"I leave it to the experts."

Damn that growl. Vincent shifted his stance. Now was not the time for his dick to wake up.

"I—"

Xavier poked him again, once for each word. "You. Are. Not. An. Expert."

Vincent slapped his finger away. "Screw off. I didn't send the report. I talked to Sydney about it, but I didn't send it. I told her I'd revise it."

"So why am I getting a phone call about potentially failing septic and a damn bridge that's barely on the property? Adverse conditions? What the fuck?"

"I don't know why," Vincent bellowed. "If you'd just fucking move, I could go see what happened!"

"Sure, I'll just step aside and let you fuck up my business!"

Unexpectedly a stab of lust swept through Vincent, leaving him momentarily breathless and reminding him of the last time he'd nearly kissed Xavier Stone. Before the flagpole incident. Afterward, Xavier had refused to acknowledge his existence.

So, instead of taking a deep breath and *thinking* about what he said next, somehow "I think you're perfectly able to mess up your own business—without my help. That ship sailed when you stripped naked and ran your underwear up the flagpole," came out instead. He really wanted to find out what Xavier's lips felt like. Why was he drawn to rule breakers?

Those golden-brown eyes flashed, and Xavier's nostrils flared. Vincent's cock twitched again, and he shuffled another inch closer to his archenemy. Maybe kissing him would be a good idea after all. If nothing else, it would satisfy a couple decades of curiosity.

A knock on the door had them jumping apart. Shooting Vincent one last death glare, Xavier stomped across the room and wrenched the door open, revealing Romy waiting on the other side. *Of course* the intruder was his own kid.

"Uh, hi." She peeked into the living room, glancing from Vincent to Xavier and back to Vincent. "There you are, Dad. Our front door is standing wide open, and I could hear you guys. I—"

"I was just leaving," Vincent said, moving quickly and grabbing Romy's arm. He practically dragged her down the steps and across the street. As they reached the sidewalk in front of their house, Xavier's door slammed shut with a boom that echoed down the road.

Romy shook his hand off her arm. "Seriously, what is up with you two, anyway?"

"Don't speak to me in that tone, young woman."

Vincent needed to take control of the conversation, but as usual, Romy was too far ahead of him.

"What tone?" she scoffed. "The one that says you like Mr. Stone and not in a 'let's go out for coffee' way?"

"I cannot stand the man." Maybe other parts of him did, traitorous parts. What was Romy doing home this early in the day?

Xavier Stone was arrogant, flashy, and a know-it-all. Just because he'd moved back to Cooper Springs after living wherever he'd been for twenty years, he thought he knew how to make something positive from the economic disaster Cooper Springs had devolved into over the years.

Which, Vincent amended, was more than anyone else in town was doing. Most of the residents seemed perfectly happy to watch Cooper Springs fade into obscurity. Except for Forrest Cooper, but he was... *Forrest*.

"Mm," Romy said as she preceeded him into the house. "What is it that old dude says? I think you protest too much? I've seen how you head to the window the minute you hear his car or see him walking past." She shook her head, obviously disgusted with his behavior. "Just get it out of your system, why don't you? We're living in the twenty-first century now, Dad. *No one cares.*"

Whether he liked Xavier Stone in a non-platonic way—*or not*—Vincent wasn't having this discussion with his too-perceptive daughter. And he totally didn't like Xavier. It was just because he hadn't had sex with another person in so long, his dick had forgotten what it felt like. He grimaced; even he knew he was acting like a teenager.

"Some people care. And my se—er, *life* is none of your business."

"Gawd, it's sex, Dad, not murder." She shook her head again as she walked into the kitchen. "Whatever. Is there anything to eat? Rehearsal was brutal today." Anyone who believed teenaged girls were light eaters had never actually lived with one or taken the drama club to Pizza Mart for after-rehearsal dinner.

"There're leftovers."

Vincent stared after his daughter, wondering when his life had become pathetic enough that he was getting unsolicited advice from a fifteen-year-old.

Not that he was taking her advice.

Shaking his own head, he glanced around the living room for his laptop. He needed to sort out the appraisal issue before everything was FUBARed.

SIX

XAVIER

"Olympic Appraisal, Sydney Baskin."

"Sydney, Xavier Stone." Xavier had practiced five long minutes of deep breathing before he made the call so, outwardly at least, he sounded calm. "What's up with the resort appraisal? Why did I get a call from the bank—which is funding only a tiny portion of this sale, I might add—about repairs to the septic system and some damn bridge?" *Breathe, calm,* Xavier chanted to himself.

There was a long silence, but he could hear a faint rustling, so he knew she was still on the line.

"Shit."

Xavier shut his eyes.

"That's why Vincent was calling. I, uh, stepped away from the desk and missed his call."

"Sydney, what happened?"

"This is my fault, Xavier," she said quickly. "Vincent called me yesterday after sending in the paperwork. He knew we wouldn't like it. I asked him to take the wording out since technically it's not his scope of work. But," she continued, her voice becoming quiet, her tone contrite, "I must have had it attached to my follow-up email to the lender, and I accidentally hit Send. God, and after telling Vincent he was on the verge of being fired! Now it's going to be me," she wailed.

Vincent was worried about getting fired? Xavier glanced out the window, feeling guilty that he'd possibly overreacted.

Okay, he had overreacted.

In the distance, a police siren started up and quickly faded away as Chief Dear, or one of his deputies, raced after a speeder on the road through town. Hopefully, it was nothing worse.

Just that morning, when he'd been on the hunt for a cup of coffee, he'd stopped in at the ancient Stop-N-Go. Unfortunately, the coffee machine had had an out-of-order sign taped on it. Instead of a caffeine fix, Xavier had been brought up-to-date on the most recent creepy people sightings, break-ins, and catalytic converter thefts. Unfortunately, Cooper Springs was experiencing the same sort of crime larger towns were these days.

"I'm so sorry. Let me talk to the broker," Sydney said, bringing him back to the present. "We all know the appraisal was merely for the final paperwork. The bank probably won't ask the sellers to repair anything." The last word ended on a distinct question mark. Xavier didn't think so either, but every lender was different.

"I'll call the buyer and see how he feels."

The words were officially on paper now, so Xavier had to inform Martin. It would be unethical for him not to. Some people —like Arsen Hollis—might *forget* something like that, but Xavier would never lie to a client. His stomach felt like he'd been drinking battery acid instead of coffee.

"I'm so sorry," Sydney repeated.

"We'll sort it out."

Xavier set the phone back down. Great, now he had to apologize to Vincent.

Dammit. The last thing he wanted to have to do was be *nice* to Barone. Like a fucking adult or something. What was it about the man that rubbed him wrong anyway? Vincent hadn't changed much in twenty years. He was still the rule-following, help-a-senior-across-the-street, rescue-all-the-kittens kind of guy. Still had the classic Italian looks of his heritage too. Only these days Vincent was stacked with muscles from doing god knew what and his dark brooding stares made something in Xavier's stomach twist.

He shook his head. Obviously, the breakup and moving back to his tiny hometown was affecting something in his brain. He needed a road trip to Seattle where he could get laid without consequences.

First, however, he needed to talk to Martin Purdy. Reluctantly, he scrolled through the landline's call log and pressed Call when he found Martin's number.

"I hope you're calling with good news," Martin greeted him cheerfully. "I already have an offer on my house and if everything goes as planned, I'll be out of the city in less than two months." The excitement in his voice was infectious and Xavier regretted that he was possibly going to ruin the man's day. Week. Month.

"Good and bad. Which do you want first?"

"The bad, tell me already."

Like ripping off a bandage. Xavier spoke swiftly. "The appraiser noted the septic may need repairing along with the bridge leading from the shellfish cleaning station out to the beach. The good news is he didn't ding the property value."

Truthfully, Xavier suspected Martin would have more trouble with Nick Waugh than the septic or a damn footbridge. The estate was a steal, seeing as the remaining Davies family members were ready to wash their hands of it.

"What's your opinion?" Martin asked.

Ugh. Xavier hated this question.

"I want this property to sell to the right buyer," he said honestly, "and you're motivated and seem to appreciate our quirky little community. But you need to know what you're getting into. It seems like I've heard septic is hard to replace, but changing out parts may be doable."

Martin was silent for a few moments and Xavier paced from his home office, out to the living room, and back. He pointedly did not look out the front window. He did not need to see Vincent Barone's face right now.

"And, I suppose, if the cabins were fully booked, having the septic go sideways would not be pleasant."

Martin was a smart guy.

"Nope."

"I probably should take some time and think about it."

Xavier held his breath, not wanting to hear Martin's next words. *It would be fine. Things would work out.*

"But I'm not going to. I want to sign on the dotted line. Moving is a pain in the ass, but I want this. It feels right."

Oh, thank fucking god, he could breathe again. Xavier had to blink a few times and replay Martin's words in his head. It really was going to be fine.

"You don't want to ask the estate to do any fixes? We could see if they'd throw in a credit for roof repair or something?"

"I suppose it doesn't hurt to ask, but it isn't a deal-breaker. The sooner this is finalized, the better I'll feel."

Too bad Martin wasn't his type, or Xavier would give him a big kiss when he saw him. This was Martin's dream, and he was going for it. Which reminded Xavier, Arsen was somewhere out in Cooper Springs, trying to steal that dream. Because being an asshole just wasn't enough of a character flaw.

"Can you drive out here today or tomorrow so we can officially sign?"

Martin agreed to be in Cooper Springs by lunch the next day. They planned to meet at Xavier's office, take one more look at the cabins, then sign everything. With a sigh of relief, Xavier ended the call. Maybe he'd pull this off.

But there was no fucking way Vincent was getting the apology he deserved until the sale was complete.

An hour or so later, Xavier was standing at the kitchen counter waiting for the teakettle to boil when his phone rang again. *What now*, he wondered irritably. But he recognized the number, so he picked up right away instead of ignoring it like he wanted to.

Why would the Cooper Springs chief of police be calling him?

"Xavier Stone?" Andre Dear's deliciously deep voice came over the line. He'd be great at audiobooks if he wasn't busy catching criminals and giving teenagers lectures about drugs and safety. He seemed like a nice guy and Xavier suspected the new chief was gay, or bi anyway, but he wasn't out. And he did nothing for Xavier. He didn't have law enforcement fantasies. Which was a pity because Andre was a lot easier to deal with than a certain shop teacher who pushed all Xav's buttons. A shop teacher he wasn't attracted to. Not at all.

"Yes?"

"Chief Dear. I'm calling because we have a situation out at the old resort."

"A situation?" Xav's heart started pounding against his ribs. It couldn't be a fire. Chief Dear would have called emergency services first.

"Trespassing, but there's conflicting information. Any chance you can come out here and clear this up for us?"

Why him? But also—Xavier supposed—better him than waiting for one of the Davies grandchildren to get there. Which would be days.

"Sure, happy to help. I'll be right there."

Grabbing his keys, Xavier shrugged his jacket on and headed out the door. He pointedly did not look at Vincent Barone's house as he drove away.

When he turned into the resort parking lot, Xavier immediately understood the problem. And he felt the slightest bit guilty about it even though Arsen was a big boy and should have read the fine print himself. It wasn't Xavier's fault Arsen hadn't believed him or Vincent. In fact, if Arsen had done *any* homework at all, he would have been aware of the situation.

Parking next to the Cooper Springs police car, Xavier climbed out and approached the waiting trio. Maybe quartet—he spotted Nick Waugh, a sentry at the top of the hill, scowling fiercely down on the group below. From where he stood, Xavier could see Nick loosely holding a wooden baseball bat by his side.

"For fuck's sake," Xavier grumbled as he reached Chief Dear's side, not looking in Arsen's direction.

"Pretty much my thought," the Chief said out of the side of his mouth. "But Mr. Waugh claims he was hired for extra security. All visitors to the property need to be approved first and these gentlemen are not on the list."

"That… person threatened me," Arsen declared.

"Did you call first?" Xavier asked, keeping his attention on Nick.

"No. The property isn't occupied," Arsen sputtered. "It's been empty for years."

Arsen's "client" didn't appear to care. Xavier wondered if he was really a client or if he was just some guy Arsen was trying to impress. The fact that Arsen hadn't done his research made Xavier even more suspicious about his true motive in Cooper Springs. Was Arsen harboring a wild fantasy that Xavier would fall at his feet and beg Arsen to take him back? Never gonna happen.

When they were boys, Wanda Stone had impressed on Xavier and Max that they needed to use their powers for good and not evil. Every day, he was more certain that Arsen never learned that lesson. Probably had never heard of it.

Xavier turned to Chief Dear. "Nick has the right to be here. The estate hired him to protect the property." Xavier spoke loudly so Nick could hear him. "Maybe not with a baseball bat"—*really, Nick?*—"but he is charged with keeping vagrants and the like from causing property damage."

"I," Arsen began, arrogance puffing his chest, "am not a vagrant."

"This guy showed up here and started snooping around," Nick yelled down at them. "Barone was already out here yesterday doing his bit, measuring the cabins and taking pictures. I heard a noise and thought maybe it was the creeper we've been hearing about." He slapped the bat against his hand and Xavier rolled his eyes.

Nick Waugh *was* a hothead. Xavier thought he'd heard Nick had been a photojournalist and was now a sculptor—of sorts—but since Nick was a tad testy, he'd never asked him about his life outside Cooper Springs. He eyed the baseball bat again. Nick had lowered it but was now swinging it at his side.

"Hollis is not a creeper," Xavier called up to Nick. "Can you imagine *this* guy sneaking around? Stand down already."

Thank you, Rufus Ferguson, for continuing to spread the creeper rumor around town. Maybe he'd have a chat with Rufus's son, Magnus, and *he* could deal with Rufus. It did amuse Xavier to imagine Arsen Hollis sneaking around town wearing his Salvatore Ferragamos and diving Rolex, peeking into windows and occasionally stealing mail. Fun times in a small town.

"Look, Arsen." Xavier faced his ex. Arsen's nose wrinkled, like he smelled something offensive. "I don't know what you're up to, but this property is basically sold. The buyer is coming into town tomorrow to finalize everything with the estate and the bank. Maybe you and your friend should tootle off to a wine tasting. It's not insect season, so you won't find flies to pull wings off of." He was done being nice to the asshole.

Arsen's eyes narrowed. The friend's face had no expression, but Xavier had the impression he was trying not to laugh.

"I don't know what I ever saw in you," Arsen sneered.

Fuck if Xavier had a clue either.

"Believe me, the feeling is mutual."

Inhaling a deep breath, Xavier stared up at the ever-present clouds overhead. He should keep his mouth shut and not antagonize Arsen any further. The clouds were dark and moody, reflecting his humor. What had he *ever* seen in this shallow, backstabbing man? Was he so desperate for company he'd taken anything he could get? Fucking pathetic.

"Mr. Hollis," Chief Dear interjected, before things could get heated again. "It sounds like you aren't welcome here and I'd rather not write a ticket because then I'll have to do paperwork. I hate paperwork." He made doing paperwork sound worse than cleaning toilets.

"By all means," Arsen ground out. "I wouldn't want to add to your paperwork." He shot Xavier a killing glance. "You can bet I won't forget about this. You've had your chance."

Chance to what, grovel? Beg Arsen to be his friend? To be a part of his life? Screw that. Xavier clenched his jaw, forcing the words to remain unsaid. His dentist would not be impressed.

There was nothing about Arsen he missed; the man held no power over him anymore. Why had he ever thought he did?

"Come on, Arsen," his friend said placatingly. "Let's head back and we can stop at that new omakase place before it closes."

Shooting Xavier one last dark look—like it was his fault Arsen looked like a fool—Arsen followed his friend back to their cars and seconds later they were gone, roaring down the road and out of sight.

"I'd follow and give them a ticket but honestly, I'd rather not," said Chief Dear.

"Paperwork," Xavier agreed.

Nick disappeared into the cabin he inhabited. Xavier stared up at Nick's "art" stacked between the cabin Nick lived in and the next over. Was that a gigantic mushroom or... something else? He tilted his head. Possibly it was a walrus. Nick's sculptures were just something Martin Purdy was going to have to live with for a year, give or take.

Xavier was about to take off when Dear's radio crackled to life.

"Dear."

"Time for you to go home, Chief."

The voice of Lani Cooper, one of the CSPD deputies, crackled over the radio connection. Lani was Forrest Cooper's younger sister. Xavier couldn't imagine being Forrest's younger sibling, or any member of Forrest's family for that matter. Forrest and Lani had spent their young lives in a survivalist household until they were rescued by their grandfather. This explained a lot about Forrest, but not why Lani had decided to go into law enforcement.

Not that Forrest wasn't a good guy. He just was an eleven on a scale of one to ten, possibly a twelve. He and Xavier had been best friends until Xavier had moved away, Lani tagging along with them when Forrest let her. Luckily, she had been in class during the notorious briefs-up-the-pole incident in high school.

Dear replied to Lani, "It's all yours, over and out."

Dusk was quickly becoming evening. Xavier sighed, peering up again at the shadowy cabins and evergreens huddled together. He needed to get everything ready for Martin Purdy tomorrow, but it wouldn't take that long. But he also didn't feel like going home and facing Vincent Barone because, like it or not, he did owe the man an apology.

"You want to grab a beer?" he asked the chief.

Dear looked surprised. But, Xavier thought, also pleased. Andre Dear had been their chief of police for less than a year—having started after a long search for someone who was both qualified and wanted to move to such an underfunded and under-staffed agency.

Xavier wondered how many friends the man had made since he'd moved, if any. Cooper Springs could be a very odd place sometimes. Residents were friendly, but on their terms. There was a big gap between having somebody lift their hand off the steering wheel and wave as they drove by to being invited for a backyard barbecue—or for a beer at the local pub.

"Do you mind if I stop at home and change out of my uniform?" Dear asked. "It can give some people the wrong idea."

Xavier laughed. "I'll see you there in twenty." He might as well stop in at the office and print out the paperwork for Martin Purdy.

SEVEN

XAVIER

The Steam Donkey Pub—Coopers Springs' locally owned watering hole—sat on the north end of The Strip, on the way out of town, a mile or so before the abandoned lumber mill. Xavier thought it was hilarious that many locals—himself included—called the two-lane highway that ran through town The Strip. As if Cooper Springs had anything in common with Las Vegas. There were only three neon signs in town and one of them was the Open-Closed sign in his mother's shop window.

Hanging a right, he swung into the mostly empty parking lot and immediately spotted Forrest Cooper's beat-up 1962 Ford pickup parked next to a banged-up white Subaru that belonged to the pub's owner, Magnus Ferguson. He knew the truck was a '62 because Forrest had vanity plates—it was his pride and joy.

Why his friend needed a truck that had been drinking age when they were young, Xavier would never understand. Forrest had converted the thing to biodiesel, and wherever he drove around town, the scent of French fries followed him. Xavier supposed it could be worse—this was Forrest Cooper, after all.

The Steam Donkey occupied one of the oldest buildings in Cooper Springs, and the structure had always been a tavern, only the name changing over the years. Xav thought Steam Donkey was the perfect name, seeing as it harkened back to the days when lumber was the town's bread and butter, and the steam-powered winches were a part of lumberjack life. One or two of the machines had been abandoned in the forest surrounding Cooper Springs, and after eighty to a hundred years, they were now monstrous piles of rusty iron with vines climbing through them, almost another form of local art. The vibrant red brick walls of the tavern building had withstood the test of time, however, and the place was one of Xavier's favorites.

Pushing inside, Xavier blinked and squinted, waiting for his eyes to adjust to the dim lighting. He loved the atmosphere here. Marble-topped tables took up the center space and custom wooden booths with ornately carved backs sat against the walls, offering private seating like an old-time saloon. The bar took up one corner and a small open space was established across from it, one that sometimes acted as a dance floor or stage. Not that Cooper Springs had a lot of bands lining up to play.

Someday they'd have bands.

He spotted Forrest and was wandering over to say hi when he realized Andre Dear was sitting across from his old friend. Forrest patted the spot on the bench seat next to him.

"Sit your ass down. How's it going? I haven't seen you in ages."

Xavier met Andre's amused gaze, noting again that the chief was a good-looking man. He had one of those faces that totally transformed from serious to kind when he smiled. And Forrest had a way of being impossible to say no to. Slipping his jacket off, he hung it on the hook jutting from the end of the booth before sitting down next to Forrest.

"So, what was the excitement at the Davies property? Andre says it's your story to tell."

Andre rolled his eyes. Forrest wasn't the only resident in town with a scanner. It probably drove the chief nuts.

"Sorry," Andre said to Xavier.

"No worries. Forrest never has known how to mind his own beeswax."

The man in question just shrugged and grinned.

"Well?"

"Arsen showed up at the property without calling first. Nick warned him and the client off—although I don't think the guy was an actual client—with a baseball bat. Possibly a little overkill. *And* he called the cops on them."

Forrest wrinkled his nose at the mention of Arsen. Being the nosy person he was, he'd grilled Xavier about Arsen when he'd first moved back to town.

"He wasn't threatening," Forrest said. "He was protecting the property. Nick takes his job seriously."

Xavier snorted and opened his mouth to retort, but a throat-clearing noise informed him Magnus Ferguson had made his way over to their booth.

"Seniors Night isn't until Sunday." Magnus's voice boomed even when he whispered. He had no trouble being heard when last call came around.

"Fuck off, asshole," Xavier said. "You're older than both Forrest and me. I can't speak for the chief."

"Please, call me Andre when I'm not on duty."

The owner of The Steam Donkey grinned back at them. "Yes, but I'm a handsome fucker, unlike you with your ugly mugs, bringing the tone of the place down the minute you walk in."

"Magnus, your love language needs a bit of adjusting. And you need a new glasses prescription, because the one you have obviously isn't strong enough. The three of us bring nothing but class to this joint." Forrest crossed his arms over his chest and raised one eyebrow at their friend. Back in the day, Forrest had had bright red hair, but it had turned a deep auburn since they were kids, and the red was now shot with gray. It gave his friend a deceiving air of maturity.

Magnus clapped a hand over his heart, assuming a heart-broken expression. "You wound me."

"Are you auditioning for Shakespeare on the Beach again?" Xavier asked him, genuinely curious. "Did the council cough up the money for it?"

Magnus glanced over his shoulder at the bar. No customers waited for service, and the few patrons already seated seemed happy enough. Midweek in the winter was always slow.

"How about I take your order and then join you for a few minutes?" he asked.

They all nodded. Ordering himself a beer, Forrest muttered something about figuring out how Magnus's ego would fit in the booth. Andre ordered the same. After an internal debate, Xavier went with his usual, a glass of white wine.

Magnus headed back to the bar to pour their drinks. Over the speakers, Carrie Underwood sang about cheating and fruity drinks.

"Add some fries," Forrest yelled over the music. Magnus nodded and stepped over to the kitchen doors to let the cooks know.

A couple minutes later, Magnus was back to set down the beers, Xavier's wine, and what looked like a lemonade for himself. Forrest's eyebrows shot up and he leaned forward.

"Is that the recipe we worked on?"

"Yep," Magnus said as he sat down next to Andre. "House-made lavender lemonade." Picking up the glass, he swirled it like it was fine wine and took a sip.

"I *knew* it would be a great addition to the menu."

Magnus sighed as he set the glass back down on the table. "Just need customers in here buying it now."

Aside from two other tables, the pub was empty. Granted, it was still a bit early. There would likely be a few more customers dribbling in for their evening meals, but it was the summer months that paid the winter bills.

"It's October. We never have visitors this time of year," Forrest unhelpfully pointed out.

"Maybe we will, once the resort is up and running," Xavier interjected. "And what about the Shakespeare? I was mostly kidding, but is it in the works again?" If it was, he would totally lord it over Daisy. She could keep her renaissance festival, Cooper Springs might have The Bard.

"I've heard they're still considering it," Magnus grumbled, "but it always comes down to money. The permit to use the beach isn't cheap. And then there's everything else. And what if nobody comes?"

Xavier took a long sip of his wine, his thoughts racing. He'd forgotten about the beach Shakespeare, and suddenly he *wanted* it. As badly as he wanted the sale of the resort to go through. If Cooper Springs was going to survive—and even grow—they needed this. They *needed* Shakespeare, as well as something else to draw visitors who thought Shakespeare was boring.

Forrest nudged him with his pointy sweater-covered elbow. "What are you thinking? I can almost see smoke coming out of your ears."

"Beach Shakespeare," Xavier responded.

"And?"

How did Forrest always know when there was an *and*?

"Chainsaw art," Xavier whispered—as if anyone but his friends were listening. "A competition, something for the anti-Shakespeare crowd. *Chainsaw Shakespeare.*"

Three pairs of wide eyes stared at him.

"Dude." Forrest breathed out the word. "That is awesome."

"What's up, cuz?" Daisy asked. The smile in her voice was loud and clear.

"I have this crazy idea, and I want to run it past you."

Tucking his phone between his chin and shoulder, Xavier

slipped out of his jacket and hung it up on the antique coat rack he'd found at a shop in Aberdeen.

"Hit me with it. Kyle and I are just hanging out at the motel having microwave pizza."

Xavier wrinkled his nose and made a gagging sound.

"That is disgusting. Never share that kind of personal information with me again."

Daisy laughed, and Xavier thought he heard her son Kyle say something in the background.

"More for us, snooty man. What's your idea?"

"Two words—no, three," he corrected himself. "Chainsaw art competition. And Shakespeare. Chainsaw Shakespeare."

For a very long moment there was no response. All Xavier could hear was the sound of Daisy breathing. A chainsaw art competition was either pure genius or the worst thing he'd ever thought of. Personally, he thought the idea was genius, but Xavier had learned to run his crazier plans past his saner cousin. His brother thought all his ideas were nuts, so no way was he asking Max.

While he waited for her reaction, he stared out his front window at Vincent's house. He hadn't seen him since accusing him of trying to sabotage the resort appraisal earlier. Xavier huffed and glared harder. He still wasn't ready to apologize, even if it was the adult thing to do.

"Like a judged competition?" Daisy asked. "With safety protocols and all that? Xavier, I think that's an incredible idea! Give me a sec, there's somewhere up here that has one. Let me see if I can find a link to send you."

"Yes, and Shakespeare on the Beach at the same time, or the week before or after, maybe."

More scuffling sounds. More staring across the street. A light turned on inside, but Vincent's car wasn't home, so it must be his kid.

Reluctantly, Xavier admitted to himself that he liked Romy

Barone. She seemed to have a head on her shoulders from what he'd experienced. And a sense of humor since she lived with her grumpy-ass dad.

Sexy grumpy-ass dad.

"Yes!"

Daisy's voice startled him out of his thoughts.

"I just sent you the link. Arlington has an extreme chainsaw carving show. And, oh, check it out, there's an auction on the last day and the city donates the proceeds to charity. Xav, I think you're onto something!"

EIGHT
VINCENT

Vincent

By late Friday afternoon, Vincent hadn't seen or spoken to Xavier Stone in days—not that he was counting the hours. Management had decided that the appraisal debacle was only *minimally* his fault, and he wasn't going to get fired. He felt slightly guilty about including problems that weren't part of his job description, but he wasn't the one who'd sent the paperwork to the bank. And after all, how often did people avoid responsibility simply because it wasn't in their job description? Too many. The attitude was a huge pet peeve of his. The world would be a better place if people took responsibility for their actions, stepped up when they spotted an issue.

Like an ancient septic system. And a creaky bridge. But he'd included that, had he?

As far as he was aware, the deal had been signed and sealed. After decades of neglect, Cooper Springs Resort had new ownership. The town had to be buzzing over it.

He hadn't even seen Stone the few—not more than ten—

times he'd caught himself looking out his window in the direction of the old Victorian.

A growl threatened, rumbling in his chest. Vincent gritted his teeth, holding it in.

The first projects were due next week, just in time for curriculum night. This was not the time for him to lose focus. Eyes, fingers, noses—they were ultimately his responsibility, and he didn't want to deal with angry parents even if their children were almost adults.

"Mr. Barone?"

Guiltily, Vincent glanced up from attempting to balance his checkbook—damn, drama was expensive, and Romy needed money for some set thing, for her costume, and to pay for the script rights. The club received no support from the school district, which left parents with the bill. This year they were producing The Addams Family, a welcome change because Vincent had seen Our Town at least ten times since starting his teaching career.

He'd purposefully placed his desk at the back of the room so he could monitor the students without looking like he was a prison guard. These kids were anywhere from sixteen to eighteen years old. They had brains and needed to learn to use them, preferably without losing body parts.

"Yes, Daniella?"

Daniella was new to Cooper Springs High. Vincent knew little about her, only that she and her uncle had moved into a house near Cooper Mansion a few weeks ago. That area was an odd little neighborhood made up of quaint older homes and a few hideous ones built in the 1980s when a developer got their hands on some vacant land. Considering how small Cooper Springs was and the intense level of gossip regarding newcomers, it was surprising he didn't know more about Daniella and her uncle.

"I was wondering, um, could I get an extension on my project?"

Daniella's fingers twisted tightly together, and she had dark circles under her eyes. She was only a sophomore, younger than his regular students. But he'd made an exception seeing as she needed the credits, and he was basically a complete softy.

He could practically feel the rest of the class listening to their conversation, even though they were supposed to be working on their own projects. Extensions were rarely given. Not because he was a hard-ass, but because students would have to come in after school or possibly the next semester to do their work. Principal Robinson got very weird about liability.

But Daniella *had* moved to town after school had already begun. And her project, started after everyone else's, was an intricate birdhouse, one of the cooler designs Vincent had seen in a while. Most of his students were lunkheads who took his class because there were no papers to write. An awful lot of cutting boards came across his desk.

"How much time do you think you need?" he asked.

"Maybe just a few days? A week?" Her eyes were wide and her gaze imploring.

Vincent could almost hear Romy's voice telling him it was okay to bend the rules sometimes. Shop wasn't rocket science. A late project wouldn't mean the end of the world.

Fine.

He tapped his desk with his finger. "This one time—because you enrolled late—I will allow it. Remember to talk to me Monday or Tuesday and we'll figure out a schedule. Don't forget you're going to have to do the project for second quarter too."

"Thank you, Mr. Barone. Thank you so much," she whispered.

The bell rang and they were both free for the weekend. The rest of the class gathered their stuff and crowded out the door.

"I'll see you next week."

.   .   .

After clearing off the top of his desk and locking the drawers that held tool keys and other things he didn't want to go missing over the weekend, Vincent checked around to make sure he hadn't left anything out. Nope. He lifted his jacket off the back of his chair, pulled it on, and patted his pockets, making sure he had his wallet and keys.

The idea that Stone could be avoiding Vincent barged into his thoughts. He paused in mid-step toward the door, set his foot down, and grunted aloud at his own idiocy. Who cared? Luckily for Vincent there were no students left in the room. Moving away from his desk, he took one last look around before stomping out of his classroom toward the school parking lot.

Why couldn't he stop thinking about Xavier Stone? His confident stance. The arrogant eyebrows with that tantalizing scar bisecting one. And those polished city looks? They were making Vincent as irritable as a spring bear. Add to that what Romy had said so offhandedly—*it's just sex, Dad*—and he was about ready to rip off some innocent person's head. As if he even wanted his kid thinking about sex—and especially sex he might have. Er, want. *Think about.*

It wasn't the bi thing, or not being out—at least Vincent didn't think so.

As Romy had so helpfully pointed out, the world had changed since he was in high school. And he had kissed other men. Once or twice. Mostly to confirm he'd enjoy it—which he had. Soon after, he'd met Carly and, unfortunately, decided it was both easier and more convenient to stick with women. His parents might not have turned their backs on him if he'd come out, but they wouldn't have understood it. They'd been very traditional, old-world Italians.

Aside from Romy being born, Carly had, hands down, been the worst choice Vincent ever made. But that choice was why he had his daughter in his life, so he'd live it all over again, every last damn bit. Although he wouldn't mind if they skipped the times Vincent had returned home from work to discover Romy playing in the front yard in the rain with no shoes or coat on. Or the time—the last time—Carly had taken Romy with her to buy drugs. Eight years later, he still had nightmares that ended with Romy being kidnapped or wandering off into the forest and being lost forever.

Remembering Carly was a lot like unsuspectingly walking through a spiderweb. He needed to shake the memories off. Maybe he'd stop in at The Steam Donkey instead of heading directly home. Romy had plans with friends, and he wanted to catch up on what the town gossips were saying about the sale of the resort. Possibly the news wasn't out yet, but he doubted that. More than anything, he craved adult conversation that wasn't teacher chatter, and he got enough of the under-twenty-one set at work and home.

But most importantly, he needed *something* to stop thinking about Xavier Stone.

Hah.

He was a damn mess.

Outside, it was fully dark already and heavy rain was falling as it had all week, but he didn't bother pulling his hood up. He jogged toward his practical gray Toyota sedan waiting at the back of the lot. The rest of the staff had already departed and his was the only car left. Vincent liked to give the older teachers closer spots and a few extra steps in his day never hurt.

Beeping the lock open, he slid behind the wheel and started the engine. As he backed out of his spot, sex with Xavier Stone still had a headliner spot in his brain.

"What is wrong with me?" he growled.

Three damn nights and his brain hadn't been able to think about anything else but sex. *Sex. Sex. Sex.* For crying out loud, he was forty-two and his body was behaving like a teenager's. He needed a good night's sleep, not sex-fueled dreams.

Specifically, not sex-fueled dreams starring Xavier Stone. Sure, morning wood was a thing, he wasn't dead. But morning wood because he'd been dreaming about Xavier Stone was a level of fuckery he didn't know how to deal with. Other than to take care of himself, which he did.

Had. Had, had, had.

On autopilot, Vincent took a left instead of a right, cursing when he remembered he was not going home. The pub was calling his name. He needed a beer. Maybe two.

This unhealthy fascination with his infuriating and unfortunately hot neighbor was officially over. Done. Wasn't happening. No way. Nope. His reaction was purely because Vincent couldn't remember the last time he'd had sex.

After Carly had left them, there'd been a period when he'd been a bit of a man-whore, but it hadn't lasted. He'd quickly realized he needed to focus on his young daughter and rebuilding their life, not... other stuff. And Vincent wasn't willing to risk his heart again. He obviously had terrible judgment—this fascination with Xavier only reinforced this knowledge.

By the time Carly exited stage left, Vincent had already known he didn't love her anymore; child endangerment had taken care of that. But he had loved her in the beginning. He wasn't risking his heart or his daughter again.

Having someone stomp on his heart once was enough, thank you very much.

The pub's parking lot was full, forcing Vincent to find a spot on the street. Maybe he wasn't the only one wanting the scoop on the resort's new ownership? It *was* Friday, but it was also winter, so the Steam Donkey being packed was not what he'd expected.

When he tugged open the back door, he was shocked to

discover Cooper Springs' version of a town hall; the place was wall-to-wall with residents. He'd missed something important. Fortunately, Vincent was tall enough to see over most people's heads and he easily spotted the new chief of police standing in the stage area. He appeared to be answering questions from the gathered crowd.

What the heck was going on?

Out of the corner of his eye, he spotted a stranger around his age leaning against the wall next to the door. Beefy arms were crossed over a black leather motorcycle jacket and his intense gaze was focused on Chief Dear. Vincent didn't recognize him, so he was new to town or just passing through.

"What's going on?" Vincent asked.

"A kid found some bones in the woods behind town," the man replied with a shake of his head.

Vincent's first thought was of the girl who'd gone missing from Aberdeen a few months ago. But what did he know? It could be anyone. The forest was a harsh mistress that many misjudged.

"They found the girl from summer?" he asked anyway. She'd disappeared—or run away—sometime in July, he recalled. Her face was plastered on billboards across the peninsula that her family had paid for.

The man shook his head. "They haven't said. Was the girl you're talking about a hiker or something?"

"No, I don't think so. Who is it, do they know?" Vincent fought the need to race home and check that Romy was okay. But, duh, he'd know if she was missing. *Breathe, Vincent.* Most of the time, he didn't care that they had little to no cell service in town but not tonight. Besides, he reminded himself, Romy was out with Violet and Char.

The man shrugged and shook his head. "No name yet, as far as I know. I don't think they've said if the remains are male or female."

"I can't..." Vincent forced himself to stop imagining it was Romy or anyone he knew. They'd find out who it was—had been —soon enough. One problem in a town the size of Cooper Springs was knowing everybody's business.

Vincent rolled his neck and breathed in through his nose, trying to dampen the automatic panic reaction. He stuck his hand out toward the stranger. "I'm sorry. We haven't met. I'm Vincent Barone. I teach shop at the high school."

"Dante Brown," the man offered, not smiling but offering his hand for Vincent to shake. "I think you have my niece, Daniella, in class."

"Oh, right, I do. She seems like a good kid."

Over the head of someone he thought was Mags Serle, Vincent kept his attention directed toward Chief Dear, who seemed to be wrapping up his talk.

"Are they organizing a search party or something? Is this why everyone is here?"

Dante shook his head. "From what I understand, this is an abundance of caution. He's asking folks to keep an eye out for anything out of the ordinary."

"Where was the body found? Who found it?"

"All I know is behind town and a kid found it," Dante said quietly. "Although what a kid was doing out there in this weather, I have a hard time imagining."

"Damn, someone is going to get some bad news soon."

"Yep."

Something about Dante Brown's tone had Vincent glancing at him, but he didn't offer an explanation. He was back to watching the stage, focused on Chief Dear.

The chief finished speaking and Vincent stepped away from the exit. A significant number of Cooper Springs residents pushed past him on their way out, whispering and talking amongst themselves about who it could be and what they'd been doing on the trail in this sort of weather. Spotting Rufus

Ferguson and Wanda Stone leaving together, he nodded at them. When he glanced back toward the door, Brown had disappeared.

He briefly debated heading home, but he didn't want to be alone where he'd just stew about the body and worry about Romy. Someday they'd have decent cell service and the phone in his coat pocket wouldn't be just a fancy way for him to check email when he was somewhere with internet service.

"What can I get you?" Magnus asked when Vincent reached the bar.

He scanned the chalkboard beer menu. "A pint of Old Growth. Thanks, Magnus."

"Coming up."

"Who found the remains?" Vincent asked. If anyone who was not CSPD would know, it was Magnus.

Magnus frowned. "Jayden Harlow. I have no idea what that kid was doing on Crook's Trail, but he flew in here a couple hours ago like a bat outta hell, babbling about a skull. He was covered with mud and freezing cold. The damn fool kid shoulda been in school." He set the pint on the bar in front of Vincent, who picked it up and stepped to the side so the next person could order.

"Jayden Harlow? What was he doing?" Magnus was right, the kid should've been in school.

Magnus raised an eyebrow and shrugged, and Vincent scowled. Zenith, where Jayden and his family lived, was on the other side of the forest. Not even a town, just a bump in the road that had been steadily losing residents since 1975. Jayden was a freshman at the high school and had a younger sister named Abby.

It was an open secret that the Harlow family struggled. Jayden's dad, Corey, was in the Navy and gone more often than not. Corey's wife, Lizzy, had been a good friend of Carly's. Which meant they'd had the same bad habits. Vincent had always wondered how those two ended up together. And whether Corey knew what happened while he was gone or if somehow Lizzy Harlow managed to clean up just enough so he wouldn't suspect anything when he was home on leave. He didn't know Corey Harlow well enough to stop him in the street and say, *hey, your wife is off the rails*, but he often wished he did.

"Damn, Jayden's lucky he's okay."

"Pretty sure he'll never forget a discovery like that," Magnus agreed.

"Has anyone been to check on the Harlows lately?" Lizzy hated Vincent so he couldn't go.

"That's where Chief Dear is headed now. Taking Jayden home and doing a sneaky home visit."

Vincent did not envy the chief's errand. Leaning on the bar and sipping at his beer, he wished humans weren't so often bent on self-destruction.

"Another chardonnay, please."

The voice was one Vincent recognized. Smooth, full of promise, and pushing aside his lingering anxiety over Jayden and the remains. How could the word chardonnay be sexy? He didn't even like wine.

Casually, he glanced at the mirror set into the backbar. *Xavier Damn Stone*. Was the universe working against him?

NINE

XAVIER

Xavier spotted Vincent Barone standing at the bar after Andre left with Jayden Harlow in tow, and he abruptly found himself in need of another glass of wine. It was past the time for him to suck it up and apologize to the man. Daisy would approve. He could almost hear her telling him not to be an ass. And his mom, too. She'd just left with Rufus Ferguson and he refused to speculate why.

Wanda had said something about Rufus being in the shop when they heard the news, so they'd walked over together to hear what Chief Dear had to say about the discovery. But that didn't explain why they left together.

Xavier fervently hoped these were old bones finally uncovered by the relentless rain. The last thing Cooper Springs needed was a new tragedy. The town was still recovering from the drowning deaths of five local fishermen, and that happened over fifteen years ago.

He felt for the kid, Jayden, who, for reasons not yet explained, had been out on Crook's Trail in the storm. Sure, Xavier had done stupid shit like that when he was a kid, but weren't kids smarter these days?

The pub had cleared out quickly. Most folks had been there to hear what Chief Dear—*Andre*—had to say about the remains and to find out if there was any chance it was the girl missing from Aberdeen. Or they'd just wanted to be first "in the know" so they could spread the news.

Squaring his shoulders, Xavier wove through the remaining crowd to the bar. The first chords of Oasis's *Wonderwall* began playing through the speakers overhead. It was Friday evening, after all.

At first, Barone didn't notice Xavier standing there, he was too focused on the pint in front of him. Had he had a hard day? Did Vincent know the kid who'd found the bones? Xavier had known Corey Harlow growing up, of course, but hadn't touched base with him since he'd moved back to town. Maybe the kid was old enough to be in one of Vincent's classes.

There was a great deal Xavier didn't know about his neighbor. He shifted his stance, wondering how best to start the conversation, when their glances collided in the mirror behind the glassware, liquor bottles, and little league trophies that crowded the back bar. Maybe clashed was a better descriptor. Had there been heat in Barone's eyes for a moment? Nope. No way.

Whatever it had been, Vincent shut it down fast.

"Yo, Xavier," Magnus complained. "Move your ass. It's nice enough, but it's in the way of me making money."

Moving to the side, Xavier ended up shoulder-to-shoulder with Vincent. Vincent stiffened and Xavier resisted rolling his eyes. The guy still had a hard-on about Xavier's overreaction. Well, it was now or never. He'd vowed to apologize, and he would.

Dammit.

"We need to talk. Let's grab a table." As the words left his mouth he grimaced. Because everybody loved hearing those four words. Maybe he should have practiced in a mirror first.

"What about?" Vincent asked suspiciously, his dark brows drawing together.

Grabbing his glass of wine, Xavier shot him an impatient look.

"Because we need to clear the air if we're going to live across the street from each other and I, for one, would like to not have some weird"—he waved one hand— "hoodoo-crap between us."

"Fine," Vincent said. He didn't sound too pleased. "Hoodoo-crap? What exactly is that?" he muttered just loud enough for Xavier to hear him.

"Hoodoo-crap is just that, the unknown," Xavier said over his shoulder.

As luck would have it, the booth where he'd joined his mom and Rufus earlier was still open. Setting the wine down on the table, Xavier picked up the empty glasses they'd left behind and carried them back to the bar. When he returned, Vincent had sat down and was watching him with a funny expression on his face. Not heat this time, more surprise, or curiosity.

"What have I done now?" Xavier demanded as he took a seat across from him.

Vincent shook his head. "Nothing."

"I wasn't raised in a barn, you know. I know how to clear the table and eat with a fork and knife. I don't leave the toilet seat up —even at my own house."

A reluctant smile curved Vincent's lips. *Nice lips.* Xavier blinked. Now was not the time to be distracted by lips, especially not Vincent's.

"Yeah, well, who wants to see into the toilet bowl every time they step in the bathroom? If I forget, Romy is sure to tell me about it."

Xavier opened his mouth, intending to start his apology, but his brain stalled out. It was those damn lips again. Hastily, he took a big sip of his wine, enjoying the oaky flavor and the smooth slide of the liquid down his throat.

Throat.

A very wrong yet extremely detailed image of his lips wrapped around Vincent Barone's cock flashed into his brain in Techni-fucking-color. He could almost hear Vincent's *hypothetical* moans in fucking Dolby surround sound.

Gasping, the gulp of chardonnay he'd just taken shot down the wrong pipe. As he coughed and tried to get his breath, Vincent rose as if he was going to come around the table and pound him on the back.

"Are you okay?"

Fuck. *Pound*. No.

"Fine," Xav huffed, waving at him to sit his ass back down. Coughing, he wiped tears from his eyes. "Just swallowed wrong."

Replay: dick and lips.

Something was seriously wrong with him. Vincent Barone had a kid. He wasn't bi. Was he? It wasn't out of the realm of possibility. Xavier wasn't bi but plenty of his friends were. Xavier had just never considered it before. Before now. Before this very fucking moment. Because this was *Vincent*. From fucking high school. High school was not a time Xavier had fond memories of.

"What did we need to talk about?" Vincent asked, dragging him back to reality.

The reality where his neighbor, who he was apparently inappropriately and inconveniently lusting after, was probably not bi.

But he could be.

His cock twitched. Shifting in his seat, Xavier went through a mental list of things that he found disgusting—runny eggs, the smell of microwaved fish, cat vomit. There. The last thing he needed right now was an erection.

Xavier still owed Vincent an apology. An olive branch at the very least.

"Oh, right." Xavier sucked in a deep breath, vowing he'd take that road trip to Portland or Seattle sooner rather than later. "I want to apologize for accusing you of interfering with my business. I'm sorry. And also, uh, thank you for playing along when

Arsen showed up the other day. But, yeah, Sydney explained that she'd unintentionally sent in the appraisal. That you'd already agreed the detail about the septic didn't need to be on there."

Smooth, buddy, so smooth. Xavier's face heated and he hoped Vincent wouldn't notice that he was blushing.

"Did everything go through?"

Vincent seemed sincerely concerned about the sale. He was leaning across the table, close enough that, even in the dim light, Xavier could easily see the smile lines at the corners of his eyes and the shadow of his dark beard. Xavier gripped the stem of his glass and took another gulp of his wine, only to realize his glass was empty.

"Well, it hasn't closed yet, we've got thirty days, but everything's signed. Martin Purdy, the new owner, drove up the day before yesterday and we got everything taken care of. So, yeah, it just needs the ink to dry. And he's calling in an inspector, so he knows where to start first with repairs."

"That's great! I hadn't heard anything yet. And frankly, I didn't want to call Sydney and ask. I just feel lucky I wasn't reprimanded again. I need the job to pay for all the stuff Romy needs, like, you know," he said, waving a hand, "braces, drama stuff, clothes."

Xavier didn't have nieces or nephews to worry about, but he did seem to remember his mom complaining that he and Max always seemed to need something, and she could never get ahead.

"We're good." Reaching across the table, Xavier covered Vincent's other hand with his own. "Everything worked out."

Vincent's eyes widened and Xavier glanced down at the table, to where he was still covering Vincent's hand. He snatched his hand away. What the ever-loving fuck? It was long past time to get out of the Donkey and back to the safety of his home.

"Okay then? We're good? I should get home," he babbled. "This old man needs his beauty sleep."

Sliding out of the booth, Xavier grabbed his wine glass and

walked it to the bar, setting it down with the other empties. Magnus shot him a WTF look. He ignored it; he had credit, he'd pay later. Magnus was the second biggest gossip in Cooper Springs—the apple hadn't fallen far from the tree. No way was Xavier telling him he suddenly had the hots for the shop teacher. This wasn't fucking high school.

Xavier drove home on autopilot. A herd of Sasquatch could have jaywalked in front of him and he wouldn't have noticed them. An hour ago, he'd been concerned about remains found outside of town, that they might possibly turn out to be the missing teen from Aberdeen. He was still very concerned about the missing seventeen-year-old, but now he'd added freaking out about his inappropriate reaction to his hot, rule-following neighbor.

Who he hated.

Right?

Because somehow single-dad-shop-teacher was his new kink. Xavier screwed his eyes shut and groaned. This was not happening.

As soon as he got inside the house, his landline rang. Glancing at the screen, he recognized his brother's number.

Fuck. He did not want to talk to Max. He picked it up anyway. There was no point in trying to ignore him.

"Hey," he said as he continued into his kitchen. He needed another glass of wine. Then he'd turn on the TV and finish the last season of Stranger Things. A nice gay night at home.

"What's going on?" Max demanded. "You sound weird."

Oh, just fantasizing about my neighbor, that's all.

"What do you mean, what's going on? I don't sound weird."

Did he?

"Yeah, that answer never worked for either of us in the past. It's not working for you today."

Double fuck. He dragged his hand through his hair, trying to quickly come up with something to distract Max. Something not about wanting to burn the sheets with Vincent Barone.

"Spit it out."

He'd been too slow. Dammit.

"Fine."

"Before I die of old age."

"I should have offed you in the womb."

"Never would have happened. I was several ounces heavier than you. Quit stalling."

Being a twin was both comforting and irritating. He'd read that not all twins had the "connection," but he and Max did. Usually at the very worst times.

"I have the hots for my neighbor I don't even like." He definitely did not like Vincent. "He's bossy, interfering, and always has to be right."

Except Vincent had updated the appraisal, so he didn't always need to be right, did he?

"Oooh." His evil twin drew out the single word, laughing like the demon he was. "We're talking about Vincent Barone, aren't we?"

Shutting his eyes, Xavier gently banged his forehead against the door jam. "Maybe."

Max's laughter was extremely irritating. Especially because it sounded *exactly* like his own. Max was going to pay for this when he started having feelings for someone. Not that Xavier had feelings. He did. Just not for Vincent. Did he?

"You're both adults. He's single, isn't he? Maybe, you know, have a conversation, see what happens."

"We just had a conversation," Xavier growled.

"Mm-hmm. Did you run away like you always do? I remember Vincent from high school. He was a nice guy back then. And I imagine he's still better than the last jerk you dated."

No one had liked Arsen except Arsen.

"He has a kid! He's not gay!"

"You've asked? And, brother, having a kid does not make you straight."

Xavier knew that. But after hating Vincent for months, Xavier was trying hard not to want to jump the guy the next time he saw him. And not being gay was quickly becoming the only reason stopping him.

"No, I haven't fucking asked. 'Hey, Vincent, even though I mostly hate your guts, are you bi? Because I can't stop thinking about you naked.' Does that sound about right?"

"For such a savvy guy, you sure can be an idiot." Max laughed again. This had Xavier clenching his jaw again. No matter what Max claimed, Xavier was pretty sure he could have taken him in the womb. "I've decided there's nothing to worry about. You two will sort this out."

There was a knock on the front door. Ignoring his brother, Xavier tossed back another gulp of chardonnay. It was too expensive to swill like a peasant, yet here he was.

"Talk to you later!" Max said, with far too much cheer.

Sighing, Xavier peeked out the front window, even though he knew in advance who he'd see on the porch.

Vincent Fucking Barone.

Vincent must've seen him, too, because he waved and held something up for Xavier to see. His jacket, which he hadn't even realized he'd left at the pub.

"Wait," he pleaded with his brother. But there was nothing but a dial tone.

Vincent was going to think Xavier uncivil if he left him standing on the porch any longer. Returning to the front door, he pulled it open.

"Hi," he exclaimed with forced joviality.

Vincent eyed him, obviously wondering if Xavier had lost his mind. "You forgot your coat. I didn't want you to think you'd lost it."

Spoiler alert: he had, in fact, lost his mind.

Opening his door wider, Xavier motioned for Vincent to come inside. Accepting his forgotten coat, he hung it carelessly on the coat rack and turned to face Vincent.

"A glass of wine for your effort? Or bourbon? I'm afraid I don't have any beer."

Vincent pursed his lips and cocked his head before nodding.

"Sure, bourbon sounds good. I haven't had any in a while."

"Neat? On the rocks?"

"Do you have lemon?"

"I do."

"Neat with a sliver of lemon."

"One neat bourbon coming right up. Come on into the kitchen."

Spider? Fly? Which was Xavier? Mostly, he felt like an idiot.

While he busied himself making his guest's drink, he watched him out of the corner of his eye. Vincent must've stopped in at the pub right after school. He was wearing what Xavier had labeled his teacher outfit—Dockers, lace-up shoes, and a practical brown sweater. Personally, Xav liked Vincent's weekend wear better: worn jeans that displayed all the goods and a seemingly unending supply of tight-fitting t-shirts.

"So, uh," he began, breaking the most awkward silence of his entire life. "Why appraisal? Are you going to stop teaching?"

Truthfully, he was curious and wanted to know more about Vincent. He'd purposefully not asked his mom to fill him in on any Cooper Springs gossip about the man. What had happened to his wife? Were they divorced? Xavier had never seen a woman visit the little house across the street.

"What? Stop teaching? Yeah, no. I enjoy teaching, but Romy's got drama club and braces are coming up. The extra cash helps out a lot."

"What about her mom? Doesn't she help out?"

Not that Xavier and Max's dad had helped them out after he'd bailed. It had been a case of good ol' Dad being there one day and gone the next. Romy must have fared better in the co-parenting department then Max and Xav.

Vincent took the drink Xavier held out to him, sipping it before answering.

This was unnerving. Usually, Xav was good at the wooing. But... he wasn't sure this was wooing, anyway. Usually, he knew if the man in question was interested and things pretty much just went from there. Surely neighbors shared an occasional drink?

Vincent caught his eye, and Xav's heart skipped a beat.

Dammit, he hadn't blushed like this since he was fifteen and first figured out that boys did it for him. Vincent's gaze dropped and his tongue darted out and passed across his lips. The temperature in the kitchen shot up, hot enough to melt rock.

"I don't want to talk about Carly." Vincent's voice sounded slightly hoarse. He set the bourbon back down and moved into Xavier's space, close enough he could feel Vincent's body heat and smell his slightly earthy scent—could be aftershave, could be lumber. Whatever it was, Xavier liked it. And so did his dick.

"What do you want to talk about?" Xav asked, leaning his butt back against the edge of the counter. God, he was bad at this anymore—Arsen fucking with him had messed him up more than he'd realized.

Vincent moved first, thank god, or they probably would have been standing there staring at each other all evening. Xavier would've gone to bed and suffered through another night of blue balls.

Their lips crashed together with zero finesse. Luckily, neither of them lost a tooth or split a lip. Xavier opened his mouth, needing to taste the whiskey he knew was on Vincent's tongue. One of them moaned, and Xavier suspected it was him. It had been so damn long since he'd felt this visceral level of attraction to another man.

Had he ever?

His fingers grasped at Vincent's ugly sweater, wanting more, wanting to feel the warm skin hiding underneath the wool. Vincent read his mind and broke the kiss to tug the sweater up and off his body. Whatever t-shirt he was wearing underneath went along with it and they both landed on the kitchen table.

Xavier blinked. He and Vincent Barone were in his kitchen, tearing each other's clothes off.

"Is this okay?" he had the bandwidth to ask. Barely.

It was Vincent's turn to blink.

"Um, yes."

Xavier wanted to ask more, like why now and why him? Was he drunk and making the right decision? But he wanted Vincent and he—selfishly—didn't want to stop. Taking his answer on face value, Xavier reached for him again, stroking his fingers through the dark mat of hair on Vincent's chest and allowing his fingers to trail down to the buttons of his Dockers.

He hesitated again, his fingers lingering on the clasp. Vincent was into this, if the bulge below was any indication.

"Yeah?"

"Yeah," Vincent said firmly.

He unhooked the clasp, pushed the fabric aside, and cupped Vincent's impressive erection through his cotton underwear. Vincent released a quiet gasp of pleasure. Had it been as long for Vincent as it had for him?

Strong thick hands gasped the back of his head as Vincent pulled him in for another brutal kiss, Xavier's hand jammed between them. While Vincent plundered his mouth, he massaged Vincent's cock, reveling in the heft of it in his grip. Vincent shifted his hips as their tongues tangled together, tasting each other. Xavier's cock twitched, demanding more.

Reluctantly, Xav pulled away.

"Not here. Upstairs. My bed," he managed.

Without waiting for an answer, he grabbed Vincent's hand and dragged him out of the kitchen and across the living room to the stairs. He wondered if he should worry about his sheets and decided that was overthinking things.

A quick glance into his bedroom told him his room was tidy, thank fuck. Leaving the overhead light off, Xavier fell back onto the mattress, pulling Vincent down on top of him.

Their mouths came together again, lips and tongues hungry for each other. They both still had on most of their clothes and Xavier wanted skin, but he didn't want to stop. Vincent's weight pressing him into the comforter, grinding their erections together, had him mindless.

It was Vincent who pulled away this time. "Clothes off." He rolled to the side and pushed his slacks down. "Damn shoes," he muttered, bending to untie them.

Xavier tore his gaze from Vincent to hastily unbutton his shirt and fling it, and his undershirt, to the carpet. He had to stand up to take off his own pants, underwear, and shoes, all of which ended up somewhere on the floor.

A choking noise had Xav glancing up. Vincent was staring at him hungrily, as if Xavier was the last hot dog on the warmer and he hadn't eaten all day. Arsen had never looked at him like that. With unabashed *wanting*.

Reaching down, he stroked himself. His cock, free of the confines of the Calvins, stretched toward Vincent.

"You like?"

"Yes, I like. Get back on the bed. Now," Vincent ordered.

In bed, bossy Vincent was hot, and Xav had no problem following his direction.

Vincent covered him with his body again. All the lonely places on Xavier's skin reveled in the contact, like dry ground soaking up rainfall after a drought. His soft body hair and the hard muscles Vincent hid under his practical teacher outfits made Xav's cock throb again. He ground his hips up against Vincent's, needing more.

Another deep groan escaped Vincent and he pressed back

against Xav, his touch just right. Wrapping his hand around the back of Vincent's neck, Xavier licked into his mouth. He was marauding, his tongue his weapon of choice, and all the while his hips moved against the man on top of him.

Xavier wasn't going to last much longer, his balls were already high and tight as the spark at the base of his spine threatened to burst into flame. A growing amount of wet—precome—pooled between them. Vincent was as hard and ready as Xavier. Breaking off the kiss, he reached between their bodies and wrapped his fingers around both their cocks. Vincent was thick.

"Oh, god, Xavier," Vincent rasped. His breathing was ragged and his hips began moving frantically.

Xavier spread his legs as wide as he could with his hand pumping their cocks together in between them. Vincent lifted onto his forearms and jacked into Xavier's fist. The silky hardness that was Vincent almost burned in Xavier's grip. He felt the first pulse and dragged his eyes up to Vincent's face. He wanted to see him come.

Vincent Barone was literally fucking gorgeous. His eyes squeezed shut as he continued driving into Xavier's hand, his expression one of pure ecstasy. With a final thrust, Vincent sucked in a breath and come pulsed across Xavier's fingers.

With a shout, Xavier followed Vincent over the edge. More come flooded across his hand and onto his stomach. He was slippery with it. Vincent stared down at him, and abruptly Xavier was nervous. Too much? Too soon? Had he liked it?

"That was incredible."

Vincent rolled off him, flopping onto his back so they lay next to each other. The cold air had Xavier's skin rippling with goose bumps.

This was the part he was bad at. This was why he dated people like Arsen Hollis. Arsen didn't stay or ask Xavier to stay. And Xavier had never wanted sleepovers.

"You're cold," Vincent observed. Without another word, he

eased off the bed and out of the bedroom. Xavier heard him in the bathroom and then he was back and holding out a washcloth.

Xavier accepted the offering. He wiped himself down and Vincent held out his hand, then left the room again.

He didn't seem to be freaking out, but Xavier was. Very quietly.

"It's a bit early to go to bed, even for me," Vincent said when he returned, "but I wouldn't mind crawling under the covers for a little while."

Not that Xav didn't want to snuggle. He did. Against his better judgment he wanted Vincent to stick around for a little while. The issue was, snuggling and pillow talk led to feelings and feelings got hurt when people left.

Despite his misgivings, he pulled down the comforter and patted the sheet, inviting Vincent to come lay next to him.

This was a terrible idea.

TEN

VINCENT

He'd had sex with Xavier Stone. *Xavier Stone.*

Okay, not SEX sex. But close enough for government work.

And he wanted to do it again. He wanted to try all the things. The vague fantasies he'd entertained over the years were nothing like the reality of Xavier Stone's amazing body and surprisingly tender kisses. A classic case of you don't know what you don't know.

Now he knew, for real, and there was no turning back.

From somewhere downstairs came the ring of a phone. Xavier groaned and turned into Vincent's side, and Vincent shifted so he could wrap an arm around him.

"That sounds like the one my parents had growing up."

"If I had to have a landline, I decided it would be old school. The phone came from Mom's shop, one of those retro ones with all the current bells and whistles, perfect condition."

The item under discussion continued to ring.

"Do you need to get that?"

Xavier seemed to tense. "No, it's my brother."

"Does he always call at this time of night?" Who knew?

Maybe they always talked at eight-thirty on Fridays. They were twins, after all.

"No," Xavier replied, his breath tickling Vincent's armpit. "He's being a pest."

The phone stopped ringing and Xavier relaxed against his side again. Vincent liked it.

"How was it growing up with a twin?" Vincent was curious. As an only child, he had no point of reference for having any sort of sibling, let alone one you shared your birthday with.

"About like you'd expect. Like having a sibling, only nosier than most. And I guess we had each other's backs—most of the time."

"I wouldn't know. I don't have any brothers or sisters."

"You want mine? Free to a good home."

"No, I'm good. So," Vincent began, "why'd you move back to town anyway?"

The phone started ringing again. Instead of answering Vincent's question, Xavier released a gusty sigh and rolled away from Vincent.

"Apparently, I do need to answer that. Don't move. I'll be right back."

Flipping the covers back, he stood up and grabbed a silky-looking robe that hung on a hook behind the bedroom door. Xavier Stone had a silk robe because of course he did. It helped to remind Vincent that, no matter if they enjoyed getting off together, they were very different people. Vincent wore a ratty t-shirt and sleep pants from 2010 around the house and his sheets weren't nearly as soft.

He'd let himself enjoy tonight, that's all. No expectations. Relaxing against the pillows—also very nice—he told himself he wouldn't listen to Xavier's side of the phone conversation. But Xavier's voice carried up the stairs.

"Hello...What? Are you okay? No, don't go inside. I'll be right there. Wait, did you call the police? Jesus Christ, Mom, of course you call the police. You aren't bothering them, that's what we pay taxes for! Wait outside in your car. I'll be right there."

By the time Xavier pounded back up the stairs, Vincent had his pants on and was pulling his sweater over his head. Xavier glanced at him briefly, not really seeing him. Jerking open his dresser drawers, Xavier dug out jeans and a pair of cotton boxers. Without warning, he dropped his robe to the floor, where it turned into a silky puddle. Vincent was unable to drag his gaze away. Xavier Stone was a damn sexy man.

Xavier Stone looked damn good dressed too. A long-sleeved shirt and thick cotton hoodie followed the jeans. Vincent hadn't seen Xavier in casual wear since they were eighteen. He did his best not to swallow his tongue.

"What happened? Is your mom okay?" Vincent asked. Xavier needed help, not ogling.

"Someone broke into her house."

Damn, their evening really was ending.

"I have to go and make sure everything is okay. Whoever it was broke a window to get inside. Um…" Xavier glanced around the bedroom muttering, "Car keys must be downstairs."

"I'll drive you."

Xavier froze, finally paying attention to Vincent. His eyes caught the low light of the room, giving them an otherworldly cast.

"Why? I mean, your house is right across the street. You can just go home and go to bed and not deal with this. It's probably nothing."

Vincent tucked that sentence away to think about later. Growing up, his family may have been small, just him and his folks, but they'd had each other and the support of the fishing community his father worked in. What kind of support had Wanda and her twin sons had?

"One"—Vincent raised his thumb—"you shouldn't drive when you're upset. Two"—he lowered his thumb and lifted his index finger—"I'm a shop teacher, remember? I'll grab my toolbox and see what I can do. Three, it's what friends do."

Xavier eyed Vincent as if he were a species of human he'd never encountered before.

Was Xavier embarrassed to be seen with him? No, that was Vincent's own insecurities pushing to the front of the crowd. Maybe Xavier wasn't used to help being offered without payback. They stared at each other for a long moment. Eventually Xavier seemed to come to a decision. Nodding, he turned and headed back down the stairs.

"You really don't have to do this," Xavier said from the passenger seat.

Christ. Was the man truly incapable of accepting help?

"Yes, I do."

He was thankful that Romy was with her friends. It meant he'd been able to grab his tools and leave again without the teen version of twenty questions.

It was only a five-minute drive from their neighborhood to Wanda Stone's house on the north side of town. She lived on a dead-end street in a little clapboard house that butted up against national forest land, and he wasn't at all surprised someone had broken in. It was a constant battle for the forest rangers to control illegal hunting and camping. The crap economy meant there were people who'd fallen through the social services net and felt like they had nowhere else to go. There were also meth heads and meth labs hidden amongst the giant ferns and mossy cedars. He felt for Mags and Critter, the two forest rangers assigned to the southwest region.

When Vincent turned the corner onto Wanda's street, he spotted the red and blue flashing lights of CSPD. He stopped behind the cruiser and Xavier immediately got out, hurrying over to where Wanda Stone waited in her front yard, her arms wrapped around herself. Vincent watched as Xavier engulfed his much smaller mother in a huge hug.

Vincent missed his parents with a dull ache that would never go away. But they were gone now, and Wanda needed his help. Getting out, he popped the trunk open but then decided he needed to check out the damage before grabbing his toolbox.

Stuffing his hands in his pants pockets, he walked over to where Xavier stood with his arm over Wanda's shoulders.

Wanda smiled weakly at him as he approached.

"I'm so sorry to have bothered you two."

Vincent smiled back. "Ms. Stone, you are no bother. What happened?"

"I don't know. Lani's inside looking around. Honestly, if it's safe for Lani Cooper to go in there, it's safe for me. And please, Vincent, call me Wanda."

"Mom," Xavier said, his jaw clenched, "Lani is a trained police officer. She knows how to protect both herself and you, if needed."

Lani—Deputy Cooper—appeared on the front porch. "It's clear! Come on in, Ms. Stone, and you can tell me if anything is missing."

Wanda started for the porch with Xavier plastered to her side. Vincent wasn't sure if he should follow, but Wanda looked back over her shoulder and beckoned him.

The front door opened to a living room that ran the width of the house. A hallway in the center likely led to the kitchen, bath, and two bedrooms. Vincent had appraised plenty of older houses in the area with this exact floorplan.

At first glance, it didn't appear there was much damage. Vincent changed his mind after he heard Wanda's gasp from the kitchen. Peering over her shoulder, he saw that the back door had been kicked, or maybe crowbarred, open and the thieves had apparently been hungry because the fridge door hung open, the remaining contents spilling out onto the linoleum. The cupboards had been rifled through as well. A glass jar of what had been honey or jam lay broken on the countertop, its contents still slowly oozing toward the floor.

"This can't have happened that long ago." Vincent pointed at the sticky mess.

Luckily, he had extra-thick trash bags in his car. He was nothing if not prepared.

While Deputy Cooper took Wanda and Xavier through the rest of the house and catalogued the damage, Vincent stayed in the kitchen taking a few notes. Wanda wasn't going to be able to stay in her home for a few days anyway.

"... this isn't up for discussion, Mom. I'm paying for a security system to be installed. You can't stay here until it's taken care of. You'll stay with me until then."

Vincent winced and rolled his eyes. Even he was smart enough to know that tone would get Xavier exactly nowhere. He busied himself taking pictures of the damage with his cell phone as they returned to the kitchen.

"I will not stay with you," Wanda informed her son. "I'll call Angie. She has a spare room."

"So do I," Xavier ground out.

"Or Rufus, he won't mind if I stay a few nights," Wanda continued as if she hadn't heard her son.

It was obvious, to Vincent anyway, that Xavier had learned pigheadedness on his mother's knee. He cleared his throat. Two pairs of amber-brown eyes shot his direction.

"I'm going to grab my toolbox and secure the back door. Wanda, if you don't want a security system—and in my opinion, they're almost useless in town because the power goes down so often during storms around here—have you considered a dog? Statistics show that homes with dogs are much less likely to be broken into."

Wanda crooked her neck, peering at him in a way that made Vincent very nervous.

"I've always wanted a dog, but wouldn't a puppy be a lot of work? I don't have the time for the right training."

Xavier looked back and forth between them as if they'd each grown a second head.

"Don't get a puppy. I bet the perfect dog is waiting for you at the shelter. But I agree with Xavier. You can't stay here until everything is secure. And, I may be wrong, but I'm guessing he'd feel better if you stayed with him."

Wanda's eyes widened as if she'd never considered that her son might be upset about the break-in too. That worry over her safety might keep him up at night.

She eyed Xavier. "Would it make you feel better if I stayed with you?"

Xavier nodded and wrapped his arm around her slim shoulders again. Over the top of her head he mouthed, "Thank you."

Deputy Cooper departed after leaving strict instructions for Wanda to let her know if she discovered anything else missing. Aside from trashing the kitchen, the thief had stolen some costume jewelry from her bedroom, a camera, and, inexplicably, several blankets.

"Probably to carry their loot in," Lani suggested. "Most likely, they'll take the items to a pawn shop, so be sure to call around and leave descriptions."

Vincent quickly got to work securing the back door and the window the thief, or thieves, had broken while Xavier and Wanda cleaned up the food, tossing it into the plastic trash bags he'd brought inside.

An hour later, the house was as safe as it would get for the night, and they'd dragged four heavy-duty trash bags to the curb.

"I hate getting rid of all this," Wanda said with a backward glance at the bags as Vincent drove away.

"It's for the best, Mom."

"I know, but it's such a waste. Whoever this was, if they were hungry, all they needed to do was ask. I would feed them."

"I know you would, Mom. I'm glad you weren't home though. What if they were hopped up on meth or something?"

Vincent shuddered, imagining Wanda confronting aggressive druggies.

"I suppose you're right," Wanda mused. "Rufus and I aren't young anymore."

Her comment was met with silence. Vincent was trying not to imagine Rufus and Wanda taking the law into their own hands. He didn't have a clue what Xavier was thinking.

"Um," Xavier said carefully, "what were you and Rufus doing tonight anyway?"

The question was met with more silence. Vincent glanced at Wanda's profile out of the corner of his eye.

Oh.

If it hadn't been dark, Vincent was fairly sure he would have witnessed Wanda's cheeks turning a rosy shade of red.

Xavier's mom and Rufus Ferguson were courting—or whatever it was called when people over the age of sixty-five dated.

"Rufus Ferguson?" Xavier sounded flabbergasted. And yeah, Vincent understood. In a town of gossips, Rufus was *The* Head Gossip. Magnus had learned everything he knew bouncing on his father's knee. Rufus also ran the local Bigfoot Society and still spent his summers hiking through the forest, looking for signs of the mythical creature.

"Don't start with me, young man," Wanda finally responded in a do-not-mess-with-me tone. "Rufus is kind, generous, and makes me laugh. He likes to read like I do and we're talking about taking a dance class together in Aberdeen. You can judge after you've got your own love life sorted."

Had Wanda shot Vincent a significant glance? Did she suspect Xavier and Vincent had—done a thing? No, no way. That had literally happened just a few hours ago. Not that Vincent didn't want more, didn't want to do it again. It was just early days though; they couldn't even claim to have a relationship. What they had between them was fragile and easily damaged.

But Vincent was intrigued enough to want to see if it could be something more.

ELEVEN

XAVIER

After two and a half nights and two full days, Xavier admitted—to himself—that he did not enjoy his mother staying with him. Vincent and Rufus had spent the weekend fixing the damage, which, in Xavier's opinion, was above and beyond. He and Vincent had seen each other, of course, but there'd been no naked fun times. Saturday night Wanda had cooked her famous fried chicken and insisted Vincent and Romy join them for dinner, but that was it.

Today—Monday—he and Wanda were heading to the shelter to see if there was a dog she might bond with. Vincent had an irritatingly good point about electronic security systems and maybe if Wanda had a dog, she wouldn't be lonely enough to date Rufus Ferguson.

Xavier shook his head at the thought of Rufus being his step-dad. *Just no.* Or worse, Magnus as his stepbrother. He couldn't repress his full-body shudder.

Burbling and huffing, the coffee maker pushed the last of the water through its system. Quickly, Xavier filled the two go-cups he had ready and made sure the lids were tight.

"Ready, Mom?"

. . .

The shelter was as depressing as Xavier had expected. At least it was a no-kill establishment, thank god, but the concrete walls and constant barking were overwhelming. He'd never been before and suspected it was because he had somehow known how hard it would be to see all the animals who wanted homes.

A very nice volunteer, barely out of her teens, took down Wanda's information and then led them both to where the dogs were kept.

"I'll be out front. Let me know if you want to take one out to the pee area," she said as she left them on their own in front of a kennel with a depressed-looking golden retriever-ish dog. The tag said his name was Lebowski and he was two years old. Lebowski's tail flopped, but he didn't approach them. His expression said he'd seen it all before.

His mom starting walking, slowly passing by the animals until they were almost to the back of the building.

"See anyone?"

"I want to take them all home," she said wistfully.

"Me too, Mom."

The kennel at the end had two dogs in it. One was a medium-sized brown beagle-pittie mix with soulful dark eyes, and the other looked like it had been spawned by the business end of a mop. The two watched them approach but stayed snuggled together on their dog bed. They too had seen it all before.

"Oh look, Xavier, the tag says they are a bonded pair and need to be adopted together. They've been here for six months already. Oh, sweeties, come here and talk to me." Kneeling in front of the fencing, Wanda whispered sweet nothings to the dogs until they couldn't resist her any longer and hesitantly moved closer to the fencing.

For the love of Christ. Xavier knew it was a done deal, he didn't need to ask his mom. The two dogs had her heart already.

Vincent was going to get a piece of his mind when Wanda came home with not one but two dogs, all because of Vincent's suggestion.

The two dogs sniffed at Wanda. When the mop licked her fingers, she gasped and cooed again, and Xavier figured they might as well get the rest of the paperwork taken care of.

Lebowski made eye contact with him when they walked past. In the lobby, Xavier asked the girl if he could take him out with the mop and the less exuberant pitty-mix. The pittie had brown fur and a white mark on his chest. The tag on the kennel indicated his name was Berkeley and, no surprise, the other one was called Mop.

He wondered if Vincent liked dogs because, after hanging out with the three dogs and watching them sniff and romp, it was clear Lebowski was coming home with Xavier. There was no reason not to have a dog, he told himself. And he wouldn't be giving Vincent a piece of his mind after all.

It was frustrating they had to wait two days for dog background checks, but Xavier supposed the shelter made sure adopters were legitimate. After filling out the forms and paying the fees, he and Wanda headed to the pet store, picking up enough food and pet supplies to stock a small country. The volunteer had suggested crating the dogs for at least the first few weeks in their new homes, so by the time they headed back to Cooper Springs, his car was packed with bags and boxes.

Vincent and Rufus were putting the finishing touches on the fixes at Wanda's house when they arrived. They'd already stopped by Xavier's and picked up the clothes his mom had brought over, plus dropped off Lebowski's crate and several hundred dollars' worth of food and toys. If he was bringing a dog home, he was doing it right.

Rufus greeted Wanda with a too hearty, "Howdy, gorgeous."

At least Xavier hoped it was his mom Rufus was talking to. "Did you find a dog?"

"I found two dogs," Mom said firmly, clearly deciding a strong offense was the best defense. "A bonded pair who need a forever home. Their names are Mop and Berkeley." She stepped past Rufus and into the house.

Rufus's gaze slid to Xavier. "Okaaay."

Xavier shrugged. He and Rufus followed Wanda into the kitchen. Vincent was pulling the last of the masking tape off the wall where he'd touched up the paint. Xavier savored the moment, watching Vincent's muscles slide underneath the tight t-shirt.

"And Xavier is adopting Lebowski," his mom announced.

Vincent's head whipped around, his dark eyebrows shooting upward as he stared at Xavier.

"You adopted a dog too?" he asked.

"I did. Am. Whatever." Xavier recognized he was feeling defensive. Why was that? Was Vincent judging him for adopting a dog?

A broad smile spread across Vincent's handsome face. "That's awesome. Romy's always on me about a dog, but our house is a rental and just too small. I know she'd promise to walk it every day, but to teenagers, every day is a different time frame than for the rest of us."

Ohhh. Vincent *wasn't* judging him. Xavier needed to stop assuming shit like that. Vincent wasn't anything like Arsen. Which said more about Xavier's dubious past choices than any possible future he totally wasn't imagining could possibly happen with Vincent.

Wanda chuckled. "I remember the time Max and Xavier begged me to buy them a turtle. Some kid at school got one, and they decided it would be the perfect pet. The next week, they thought they wanted a snake. I took them to the reptile farm over by Elma at feeding time. They never asked again."

"Mom," Xavier protested. "That was so mean of you. All you needed to do was tell us they ate their food live." To Vincent and Rufus, he said, "Max and I both had nightmares for weeks."

"Speaking of which," Wanda said, "Max is thinking about coming for a visit next weekend."

"Why? He was just here."

Not that he didn't want to see his brother, but after the break-in on Friday, Xavier had spent an hour on the phone with Max, assuring him that everything was fine. Max was supposed to be getting ready for his trip to Wyoming, not randomly stopping in. Xavier didn't want to talk about the trip; Max knew how Xav felt about it already.

More importantly, things between Xavier and Vincent were fresh, new, still evolving, and he didn't need Max sticking his nose in his business. Had it been an alcohol-induced one-off? Vincent wasn't acting like having sex with a man freaked him out, but maybe he was really good at hiding his emotions.

Xavier thought back to their disagreement over the resort appraisal and mentally shook his head. Vincent was not an emotion-hiding person, he was a hang-it-all-out-there guy. Maybe it was Xavier who hid his emotions. Which was also something he didn't want to analyze.

"If Max comes, he may stay over Saturday night and head to Wyoming Sunday." His mom's voice dragged Xavier back to the moment. "If so, he'll stay with me. We'll have dinner together and then see him off in the morning. Besides, this way he gets to meet Mop and Berkeley before he leaves."

"Great, let me know," he said with a shrug, thankful his brother wouldn't be staying in one of his spare rooms. "I'll see you in a couple days."

Wanda smiled and stepped close to wrap her arms around him. "Thank you for driving today. I can't wait to bring the new family members home."

Xavier squeezed her back. "Bye, Mom."

He wasn't sure what to say to Vincent, so he sketched out a wave that included both Vincent and Rufus and headed to his car.

Xavier had been back home for about an hour, some of that time spent aimlessly wandering from the kitchen to the dining room and into the living room, when there was a knock on the door. Was it possible to know his visitor's identity just by the timber of their knock?

He didn't bother looking out the window to see who it was, just to the test the theory that he didn't need to peek. Sure enough, he opened the door and found Vincent waiting on the other side.

"I was just—"

Xavier cut off whatever he'd been about to say by grabbing the front of Vincent's sweatshirt, pulling him close, and planting a desperate, needy kiss on his lips.

Vincent pushed him back inside and kicked the door shut, not once stopping the kiss. Xavier's shoulders crashed back against the living room wall. One of his framed photographs vibrated from the impact. Xavier was hard as steel already and based on the way Vincent was grinding against him, he was just as aroused.

If they didn't get their clothes off, Xavier for one would be coming in his jeans.

"Clothes... off," he panted against Vincent's mouth.

Vincent reacted by kicking Xavier's legs further apart, dropping to his knees—thank fuck for the area rugs—and popped open the buttons of Xav's jeans.

"Is this okay? I've been thinking about tasting you all weekend."

Xavier nodded, speechless.

With more finesse than Xavier expected—maybe he needed to quit thinking he knew anything—Vincent tugged his jeans down past his ass. And then his briefs. Xavier moaned as his cock unfurled, expanding. Just thinking about Vincent's mouth on him had Xavier shaking with want. Vincent looked up through his eyelashes, maybe the tiniest bit vulnerable.

"Put your mouth on me," Xavier begged.

Shuffling closer, Vincent wrapped his fingers around Xavier's cock and dragged his tongue up the length of him. When he arrived at the head, Vincent's lips parted and he took Xavier inside.

Xavier wanted to watch—blow-job porn was his favorite—but his eyelids refused to cooperate. Vincent sucked, lapped, and licked. Then the hand that wasn't jacking his cock wormed its way to Xavier's rock-hard balls and lightly squeezed.

"Fuck!" Xavier's hips jerked forward, his cock hitting the back of Vincent's throat. He flailed, not knowing where to put his hands. He wanted to thread his fingers through Vincent's thick hair, but didn't know if that was okay with him—some guys hated it. Forcing his eyes open, Xavier looked down. Vincent's cheeks were concave from his effort, and Xavier traced his index finger across one rough cheek's five o'clock shadow. It was his cock in Vincent's mouth. His cock that bumped against his fingertip. With another groan, his balls tightened, and he couldn't stop himself from releasing down Vincent's throat.

Vincent pulled off him with an irritatingly evil grin. Two could play that game. Reaching for him again, Xavier hauled Vincent to his feet, swiveling to crush him against the wall this time, and claimed those plush lips. It was intoxicating to taste himself on Vincent's tongue. Xavier held his head in place so he could plunder that mouth the way he'd been fantasizing for two long days.

"Xavier, please, naked."

Xavier blinked. Vincent's handsome face was slightly out of focus.

"Yes. My room."

Laughing like horny teenagers, they raced up the stairs to Xavier's room. Their clothes ended up all over and Xavier didn't care. He howled with laughter when Vincent's foot got stuck in his jeans and he jumped around to shake them off, his erect cock bouncing as he fought with them. Xavier needed a minute to recover from the blow job, but he'd be coming again. Lube, check. Condoms? Both in the bedside drawer. Another laugh escaped.

He flopped backward onto the mattress. Finally divested of his jeans, Vincent stalked toward the bed and crawled onto it.

"You think this is funny?" he growled, sending shivers of want down Xavier's spine. "It's going to be hilarious when you're coming so hard you can't see, and this golden cock is owning your ass."

"Golden cock? Is that your idea of pillow talk?" Xavier managed to ask once he'd stopped snickering again. "It needs some work. Maybe you should take some tips from me."

Admittedly, he'd already come so hard he couldn't see.

Vincent crawled up his body, his thick erection brushing across Xavier's abs, his chest, his chin.

"Suck me, but I don't want to come until I'm inside your ass."

"Bossy much?"

"I can be bossier," Vincent assured him.

His hands gripping Vincent's hip, Xavier stuck out his tongue and swiped it across Vincent's cock. He was rewarded with a low moan rumbling deep from Vincent's chest. A drop of precome pulsed onto his tongue. Xavier loved the taste of him. He wanted to deep-throat Vincent, show him what he could do. But he also wanted Vincent to fuck him. So he stuck to sucking his tip, pulling the mushroom head barely into his mouth, licking around it and releasing it again. Then doing it again. And again.

Vincent shuddered and pulled away, sitting back on his haunches. "I need to be inside you now. Can we do that?"

Fuck yes.

Rolling onto his side, Xavier pulled open the nightstand drawer.

"Condom? I test regularly and am negative, but..." He shrugged.

"I need to get tested," Vincent said with utter sincerity. "The last thing I want to do is accidentally pass something along. Not that I think I have anything. But better safe than sorry."

Only Vincent Barone would use the phrase *better safe than sorry* in the midst of sexy times. Smiling, he handed over the tube of lube and a condom.

"Better well-lubed than sorry," Xavier quipped before rolling over and raising his ass.

"Oh my fucking god," whispered Vincent.

"Pretty much a work of art," Xavier agreed.

There was the crinkly sound of the condom package being ripped open, then Vincent said, "It's a damn good thing you're so modest."

"Eh, modest never gets a person anywhere."

The cool slick of the lube dripping onto his hole distracted Xavier and, less than a second later, it was followed by Vincent's thick but gentle touch. Blow-job porn was great, but Xavier had learned early on that he was an ass man. As in, his ass and his partner's cock coming together for a glorious experience.

"This okay?" Vincent asked.

Right, because even if they hadn't talked about it, Xavier suspected this was Vincent's first time.

"Don't you dare stop. I'll tell you if it doesn't feel good."

Vincent massaged the lube around Xavier's hole, making him spread his knees and arch his back.

"Promise? I don't want to hurt you."

"I promise."

Why did one word make Xavier feel like he'd bared his soul? He didn't have time to worry about it because Vincent chose that moment to press his finger inside Xavier.

"Oh. My. God. More, don't stop, please don't stop," he begged. His cock was coming back online, ready for more.

Vincent was excellent at following instructions. He slowly and inexorably pressed inside, opening Xavier's ass, preparing him for his cock. Instinctively, Xavier pushed backward further onto Vincent's finger, demanding more.

"More, another finger."

Vincent added a second finger, and Xavier's cock pulsed, and even though he'd come only a half hour before, he dripped onto the sheet. Vincent owned him. Vincent twisted his fingers and pressed inward, brushing across Xavier's prostate.

"Yes, yes, yes. There."

"Like that, do you?"

Vincent's thumb stroked around Xavier's entrance, tracing his hole as his fingers relentlessly moved back and forth across the sensitive patch of nerves. Xavier's cock hung between his legs, heavy, throbbing, so fucking hard—he needed to come, all he'd need to do was brush against the sheets and he'd find his release.

Vincent must have suspected—or was just as needy as Xavier —because he gently removed his fingers and a second later tapped Xavier's entrance with his cock.

"Ready?"

"Yeah," Xavier mumbled, "so fucking ready already."

Vincent mumbled something but Xavier's ears had stopped working. His cock slid past the first ring of muscle and inside Xavier's ass like a ship coming home to dock, and they both groaned. Vincent's cock was both thick and long. As he pushed inside Xavier, it skimmed against his prostate. Sensation over-whelmed him, reducing Xavier to a gibbering mess of *fuck me harder, fuck me more, don't stop fucking fucking me.*

Sweat dripped from his forehead and down his nose, his arms shaking from keeping himself in place, and the spark at the base of his spine ignited. Jamming his ass backward so he was impaled by Vincent's erection, Xavier's balls emptied again, come spurting out his cock, and he shuddered as his ass flexed around Vincent.

Behind him, Vincent released a guttural groan and pulsed into the latex. Xavier wished there was no condom between them; he wanted to feel Vincent's come in his ass. Something else he wasn't going to think too deeply about right now.

The sound of their heavy breathing filled the room.

"Holy moly," Vincent whispered. "That was incredible."

Carefully, he pulled out and rolled onto his back. Unable to hold himself up any longer, Xavier sagged onto the mattress and the quickly cooling puddle of come.

"I think you killed me," Xavier mumbled into his forearm.

"I killed you," Vincent protested. "What about me? I'm pretty sure you ruined me."

"Like ruined as in a Victorian lady? Or ruined as in my ass is the best?"

Rolling his head and aiming his dark gaze at Xavier, Vincent replied, "Just ruined as in nothing else will measure up."

Possibly sensing Xavier was working up to a freak-out, Vincent sat up and took the condom off, then walked—naked—to the bathroom. The sound of running water reached his ears, then Vincent was back with a washcloth for Xavier. When he'd finished wiping down, Vincent plucked the washcloth from his hand and took it back to the bathroom.

He hesitated at the end of the bed when he returned, as if he wasn't sure if he should stay or figure out where his underwear had ended up. Against the muttering of his inner demons, Xavier patted the mattress. Vincent graced him with a broad smile before climbing in to lay on his back next to him.

He'd rarely stayed the night in Arsen's bed, only when they'd vacationed together. It had been Xavier's choice not to. He chuckled, remembering when he told Arsen that Vincent's house was flooded.

"What?"

"I can't believe you went along with me when I made up that ridiculous story about your house being underwater."

"You had this panicked expression, I couldn't let you down. And besides I didn't like the look of the guy."

"Well, thanks."

Neither of them said anything for a few minutes, just lay next to each other *being*. The quiet wasn't uncomfortable. Just... quiet.

"So." Vincent broke the silence. "A dog, huh?"

TWELVE

VINCENT

If Vincent had any luck at all, Romy would never know that he had fallen asleep at Xavier's until oh-dark-thirty, when he'd woken in a panic, jumped out of bed, and dashed across their street, barefoot, clutching his sweatshirt to his chest like the last remaining heroine in a slasher movie.

He was not that lucky.

A sleeping Xavier had mumbled something that hopefully wasn't him being mad that Vincent was leaving. After school was out, he planned to track Xavier down and they could talk. Or not.

"Hey, Dad. Where were you last night?" Romy asked as she came into the kitchen a few hours later.

He'd had two hours to come up with something and he'd come up with absolutely nothing. Vincent was a terrible liar. It was as if he had some kind of internal sensor that started going off when he tried. He stuttered, his cheeks heated, and his skin twitched—apparently no one could see him blush, but Carly had probably lied about that too.

"Oh, um, just hanging out with a friend. Lost track of time." Smooth. He choked back a curse when he realized his fingertips were tapping restlessly against the tabletop and quickly jammed his hand into his pocket.

Grabbing a bowl from the cupboard, Romy began pouring cereal into it. Vincent let out a noiseless sigh of relief. After she'd topped the bowl off with milk, she turned his direction, staring at him as she set her breakfast on the table.

Crap. He'd let his guard down too soon.

Eyeing him, Romy drew her dark eyebrows together— his daughter had a high-quality bull-crap detector and it was on full alert. He managed to resist shifting in his seat like a ten-year-old.

"On a Monday night? When it's not a holiday?" Her eyes narrowed. "What happened to that early-to-bed thing you nag me about all the time?"

Lifting his coffee mug to his lips, Vincent shrugged as he took a big sip so he wouldn't have to answer right away. He also resisted the urge to point out she was his daughter, not his mother.

Her eyes narrowed further as her gaze moved to... his neck? He squirmed, standing up so whatever she thought she saw wasn't visible. His kid could be as—er, *informed* as she wanted to be about sex, but Vincent was a private guy and not about to share his extra-private life with his almost sixteen-year-old. Not ever.

Turning his back to his inquisitor, Vincent fished his lunch bag out of the fridge and then busied himself transferring fresh coffee into his *Cooper Springs is for Lovers* travel mug. Probably left over from the 1990s, it had a tacky graphic of two hairy Sasquatches kissing with little hearts floating above their heads. He'd picked it up at the thrift store last summer for a dollar, thinking it was hilarious. Romy had just given him a disdainful look when he'd proudly showed it to her.

"Do you need a ride in today?" Please god, not today. A car ride would inevitably lead to more questions. Vincent crossed his fingers out of Romy's sight; Romy's friend Violet had her license and a car.

"No, Vi's picking me up in a few minutes."

Vincent breathed a sigh of relief.

"Well, finish your breakfast before you leave, and don't forget your club stuff. I am not coming home to get your things for you."

"Yes, Father."

Romy shoved the last spoonful of cereal into her mouth, continuing to eye him with suspicion.

"And lock the door on your way out. I've got a meeting with Jensen this morning, so I gotta get going."

Grabbing his backpack, coffee, and lunch bag, he headed toward the door, but had a feeling he hadn't escaped quite as easily as he hoped. Romy wouldn't forget this.

"Don't forget there's a game Friday!" she called after him as he twisted the door handle.

How could he forget with his daughter, the high school, and most of the population of Cooper Springs spending the week reminding him?

"I'll be there. I promised I would be."

"And bring a friend!"

A friend? Like who? Most of the town would be there anyway. This was Cooper Springs High's chance to beat Elma High, their closest rivals. Did she mean Xavier? No way, Xavier was not a Friday-night-high-school-football-game kind of man. Vincent chuckled, imagining Xavier wrapped up in a parka and rooting for the Cooper Springs Fighting Sasquatch football team in the pouring rain.

Yeah, nope.

Outside, the weather was cloudy, but no rain—not yet anyway. However, the weather report promised more was on the way. It was that weird time in late fall, when most of the deciduous trees were bare and the rest looked depressed, just waiting for that last leaf to drop. Vincent couldn't stop himself from glancing across the street, but Xavier's house was still dark.

If only Romy hadn't already been suspicious. And he hadn't been running late. And he hadn't made sure Xavier's front door was locked before leaving. If all that hadn't happened this morning, Vincent might have snuck back over and left him a note. But Romy was probably watching him through the front window and Stuart Jensen, head of the eleventh and twelfth grade teaching staff, did not like it when his staff was late.

It was pure luck that Vincent didn't have to change his "1024 days without an incident" sign to "0 days" by the time school was out. Every time he allowed his body to stop moving, his brain started thinking. Thinking that inevitably centered around what he and Xavier had done, were doing, and how he wanted to do it again. And how he suspected he might like posh Xavier Stone more than he should, and how that could be a problem.

Not for Xavier, but for Vincent. Vincent was store brand cornflakes. Xavier was the organic kind that never went on sale. Vincent had a kid. Yes, loads of LGBTQ people had kids, but Xavier decidedly did not have any. Vincent barely made enough money to keep the roof over his and Romy's heads—hence the appraising. Xavier liked expensive things and could afford them. His silky robes in the evening, the gleaming BMW that needed detailing once a month to keep the effects of their coastal weather in check, the suits so sharp they were dangerous. His monthly dry-cleaning bill had to be more than Vincent's rent.

"Mr. Barone?"

Crud, he'd done it again. Shaking his head and glancing up, he realized Daniella Brown stood in front of his desk as the rest of the class was filing out.

"Daniella, how can I help you?"

Were Xavier and Wanda picking up their new canine family

members today or tomorrow? He couldn't remember, but something made him think it was tomorrow. Did Xavier realize the fence in his backyard was ancient and a curious dog could easily escape? Did he have time to run over and check before dark? If he remembered correctly, there was a section in the very back that had blown over last winter and only been minimally propped up.

"Um, you said to stop by to figure out when I could finish my project?"

Not the time to worry about mending Xavier's fences.

"Right. You said maybe one or two weeks, so you're estimating another... five or six sessions?" While he taught full time, shop class was on an irritating alternating bell schedule, making it hard to be flexible about project dates.

Vincent had had a fluffy dog growing up and all his mom had done was complain about cleaning up the dog hair. Did Xavier realize how much they could shed? His suits were going to be a mess. Was he ready for dog hair?

Daniella nodded, biting her lower lip. Vincent smiled, pushing dog worries to the back of his mind. *Not thinking about Xavier, or dogs, or fences.* He could maybe stay late a couple days if he shifted his appraisal commitments around.

"Are you doing any extracurricular activities?"

"No, not yet. I was too late registering," she said quietly.

Ah, the perils of moving to a small town and enrolling after school had already started. Vincent was aware whatever the reasons were, they were nothing a teen had control over. He made a mental note to ask Romy if she and Daniella had the same lunch period and if she would reach out.

"How about after school on Mondays and Wednesdays for a couple weeks? But if it's not finished by the end of the semester, I'll have to give an incomplete."

Daniella nodded vigorously, her brown hair flopping into her face. "Thank you so much, Mr. Barone. I just want it to be perfect. I promise I'll finish."

She left the room, trailing after the last of his six-period students—Brent and Jose never paid attention to the ten-minute class warning—while Vincent wondered who she wanted her bird house to be perfect for.

He'd planned to track down Xavier after he left the campus, but the instant he turned on his cell phone he had a message from Sydney. Best laid plans and all.

"We need a quick appraisal. Double your normal rate if you can get out there by six and have the report in by nine tomorrow morning."

Double his rate? He'd have to finish tonight, and he was already tired, but he wasn't turning this job down. Another few dollars for Romy's new tool kit and to toss at bills.

"Give me the address. I'll head that way now."

"I knew you'd come through, Vincent." She rattled off an address that was on the south side of Aberdeen. Damn, it was going to be almost five before he got there, but it couldn't be helped. Sydney could've called one of the other appraisers and she'd chosen him instead, which made him feel a little more confident they weren't going to change their minds about firing him. He'd have to catch up with Xavier when he got home.

Vincent finally arrived home after eight. He was famished, grouchy, exhausted (that one was all Xavier's fault), and muddy. The property Sydney'd sent him to was a mess. The overgrown yard meant he'd had to clomp around as it grew dark, taking measurements with a flashlight, and the foul interior had made him instantly wish he'd brought a face mask.

He needed a shower. His skin rippled at the thought, desperately wanting the grime off—hopefully he wouldn't develop a rash. Vincent also had the unnerving feeling he was forgetting something important, but for the life of him he couldn't remember what it was.

Releasing a sigh and opening the car door, he climbed out.

"Hey, Vincent. How's it going?"

Startled, he turned toward the property to the left his house. How he'd missed that Liam Wright was working—under flood-lights—in his self-designed outside studio, Vincent couldn't explain.

"Liam," he said moving closer to the fence, curious to see what Liam was working on.

"Working late?" Liam set his chainsaw down and pushed up his safety googles before reaching to brush off the hunk of wood that was morphing into a... large fish?

"Yeah. Uh, what's that gonna be?"

Liam pursed his lips as he too gazed at his creation.

"A merman."

Vincent cocked his head, trying to make his brain see a merman. Which part was going to be mer and which part man?

"Not a mermaid?"

"Nah, a merman, for sure. Ari the Little Merman. I'm gonna do a series. Alex in Wonderland. Cinderfella. Snow White—but, yeah, with a guy about to bite into the poisonous apple. That kind of thing." Liam looked thoughtful. "I might do a Sleeping Hunk too, or maybe a *Rapunzel*."

"Huh. Liam?" Vincent hesitated for second but then contin-ued, "Ah, are you gay?"

He had no clue about Liam. He'd known him all his life, and now they were neighbors, but he'd never known Liam to date anyone at all. Vincent didn't normally care who people slept with, but Liam's choice of sculptures had him curious.

"Why?" Liam asked. "Because I'm creating male princesses?" His face split into a wide grin. "Hell, yeah. Gay all the way."

Liam was an imposing six and a half feet tall in sock feet with a head of messy blond hair. He dressed like a fashion holdout from the nineties—Romy's words—when flannel was the height of style. Admittedly, flannel had never gone out of fashion in Cooper Springs, much to Romy's chagrin.

"I'm bi," Vincent spit out, immediately embarrassed. Did he need validation from Liam? Could he be any more awkward?

"I figured as much after watching you do the jog of shame this morning." He waggled his blond eyebrows suggestively, clearly interested in details.

Groaning, Vincent stared up at the stars. Or what would be stars if it wasn't dark out and they weren't hidden by clouds.

"You saw me? What were you doing up?" He wasn't going into any detail about what he and Xavier might have been up to. Definitely had been up to.

Shooting Vincent a knowing look, Liam let him steer the conversation away from why he'd been seen leaving Xavier's house at four that morning.

"Couldn't sleep. I thought I heard a noise but when I got up to look, I didn't see anything. Then I got this idea"—Liam gestured at his almost merman—"and decided to sketch it out. Then I had to see if I could source some wood for it. Got lucky. Dickie Paulson is clearing stumps off his property and some of the wood is usable. He even gave it to me for free—as long as I picked it up."

"Nice." Vincent's front door opened, and Romy stuck her head out, a *what are you doing* expression on her face. "Gotta go," he said, nodding toward his house. "I have an appraisal to write up tonight. Good luck with the carvings."

"Stay cool, stay bi." Liam waggled his eyebrows again. Picking up his chainsaw, he circled around his creation.

That shower was still calling Vincent's name.

"Hey, Vincent," Liam called out.

Vincent paused and turned to look back at his neighbor, who raised his chainsaw like a trophy.

"If you ever need to talk, you know where to find me."

Tugging his safety goggles back over his eyes, Liam went back to work. The burr of the saw seemed loud to Vincent, but Liam was good about not working past nine when quiet hours went into effect. Liam wasn't paying attention to him any longer, but Vincent nodded anyway before continuing his way inside.

THIRTEEN

XAVIER

Vincent Barone had snuck out of Xavier's bed, and house, in the dark of night.

Without saying goodbye. Without leaving a note. Without bothering to text.

Great, just great. How to make Xavier feel like crap in one easy step. Nothing like someone having his first all-the-way man-on-man experience with a guy and high-tailing it out of the bed as soon as he could afterward.

And dammit, Xavier had a hunch he might actually like Vincent. They were opposites in many ways, but couldn't that be a good thing? Sure, Vincent was a rule follower, but for the right reasons. Being a single dad couldn't be easy, and he and Romy seemed to have a great relationship. Vincent was detail-oriented where Xavier tended to look at the big picture.

Ugh.

Snatching his coffee cup off the kitchen counter, he took a too-hasty sip of the hot liquid. It burned down his throat in much the same way Vincent leaving without so much as a "That was a mistake" was giving him heartburn.

Xavier had to live across the street from the guy and see him almost every day. Watch him manhandle sewer covers in the rainy season and garden shirtless in the summer. Was a hookup gone wrong excuse enough to sell his house and move to another city? Maybe even state? He—Xavier, to be specific—obviously had terrible taste in men. It must be genetic. He wondered how Max managed to avoid the gene.

No. He was done running. Done moving when things didn't work out. He was adopting a dog.

Max had never been in a serious relationship, as far as Xavier knew. He didn't think his twin would be able to hide something big like that from him. Maybe they were both stunted from growing up in the *old* Cooper Springs and their Dad deciding they just weren't good enough to stick around for. It wasn't as if Mom had been able to afford therapy—hell, there'd been weeks when the only food in their house came from the past-pull bin at the grocery store and the kindness of Wanda's friends.

He glared at his house phone, but the thing didn't ring on command. Then at his cell again, which wasn't offering up any texts or calls, the same as the last fifty times he'd *accidentally* checked it. This sense of unease was why he'd sworn never to be someone's bi-curious experiment again. Been there, done that. Too many times to count.

Yesterday morning, following Vincent sneaking out of his bed, he'd felt forgiving about him leaving, if a little depressed. It had been a while since a partner had just ditched without so much as a "Thanks for the fuck," but Vincent had probably wanted to be home for Romy. Fine, check. Today, however, Xavier was done. Vincent had had his chance.

He took another sip of his coffee, carefully this time. The bitter liquid was still too hot, but he felt like punishing himself for being an idiot.

Positive thoughts, he reminded himself. He and Mom were picking up the dogs this afternoon and Xavier felt like a little kid. He was jittery and excited about bringing Lebowski home. He'd prepared his car the best he could, covering his back seat with an old blanket and snapping in one of those pet safety harnesses specially designed for car travel. He hoped it was enough. Lebowski deserved the best life and Xavier was going to give it to him.

Next on his list was finding an excellent dry cleaner for his suits.

He kind of didn't care though. Or he cared *less*. The always-casual code of Cooper Springs was starting to seep back into his wardrobe. Not that he was trading in his suits for jeans and a Carhartt hoodie anytime soon, but a little dog hair wouldn't kill him. However, he probably also needed to think about trading in the BMW, and that acknowledgment came with a twinge of sadness. Cooper Springs was not a BMW town, and it was ridiculous of him to spend as much as he did on its upkeep.

Grabbing his car keys and the dog collar and matching leash he'd purchased, he jogged out to his car. Even the mistake named Vincent Barone couldn't ruin his day.

"You're awfully quiet," observed his mom. "Is everything okay?"

"Fine. Just, ah, going over everything in my head. A dog is a big responsibility."

"Mmm," she responded.

Mmm? What did *mmm* mean? He forced himself to keep his eyes on the road.

"What?" he asked.

"Are you sure you're not thinking about that hunky and sweet Vincent Barone?"

Of course he was thinking about Vincent. But he wasn't talking about his man troubles with his mother. Never happened when he was younger and not happening now.

"Why would I be thinking about Vincent? He's just my neighbor." His mom thought Vincent was sweet. He was doomed.

Another, "Mmm."

Xavier clenched the steering wheel. He recognized that sound and knew it meant Wanda was about to tell him something whether he wanted to hear it or not.

"Maybe try that line on someone who is not your mother and hasn't known you for over forty long years. Long, arduous years. Also, I have perfectly good eyesight. What is going on between the two of you?"

Xavier sighed, focusing on the road ahead as he formulated his response.

"Fine. We slept together and he left. Nothing since then." Other than spending his entire weekend fixing the damage to Mom's kitchen. Get a grip, Xavier.

"It must be serious if it upsets you this much. Don't forget that Vincent is a busy man with a full-time teaching job, a teenaged daughter, and a part-time job too." She laughed, adding, "You have no clue what my schedule was like when you and Max were Romy's age. If I wasn't talking the principal out of throwing the book at you, I was cooking, cleaning, or working. Not in that order. Sometimes I slept."

These were all things that Xavier had reminded himself of over the past day and a half. Which perversely pissed him off because he *knew* Vincent was busy and had a kid and a life.

"He could've called or texted." The cell service in the area was just spotty enough that sometimes Xavier's texts would load like he'd just won at slots.

"Does he have your number?" Mom asked. "Do you have his? Since you live across the street from each other, it seems like you might not have exchanged numbers."

Xavier did not glance over at his mom. If he did, he would have to admit that he did not have Vincent's number and had never given him his. First of all, they supposedly hated each other. And second, they could see each other's houses, they didn't need to exchange numbers. Not when they could just jump in bed together.

"He could have crossed the street and knocked on the door," he said stubbornly.

"So, he doesn't have your number—at least, as far as you know."

He shook his head, not looking at his mother.

"No."

"Funny thing." Out of the corner of his eye, Xavier saw his mom pull her purse into her lap and dig out her cell phone. "I happen to have Vincent's number. He gave it to me when he was repairing the damage from the break-in. He wanted me to have it in case I found anything else that needed fixing. Would you like me to send it to you?"

There was no honey as sweet as Wanda Stone's knowing tone.

"Yes," he ground out. "And thank you."

His phone chimed and Wanda settled back into the passenger seat after tucking her phone back into her bag. Without looking, Xavier knew she had a smug expression on her face.

"I love you, Xavier. Don't let the fear of someone leaving keep you from pursuing a relationship. Unlike Arsen, Vincent Barone is a fine young man. I think he'd be good for you, and he's into you. That's obvious."

Into him? Could his own mother please not use that term? Vincent sure had been into him the other night. His cheeks heated, and he hoped Wanda didn't notice.

"Obvious? How is anything obvious? Why didn't he at least let me know he was leaving? Or, I don't know, leave a note?"

Dear Xavier, thanks for the fuck, Vincent. Nope, Xavier had never heard Vincent swear. *Dear Xavier, thanks for the good time.* Much more likely.

"Maybe, like you, he panicked a bit? Maybe you need to talk to him? Maybe he has a fifteen-year-old and didn't want to make the walk of shame in front of her. Don't make Vincent do all the work, Xavier, and don't punish him for leaving until you find out why. He's not like your father. Vincent stayed in Cooper Springs even when he could have left and started a new life after that wife of his took off and left him to deal with her bad behavior. Vincent is a stayer."

It was Xavier's turn. "I guess."

Vincent *was* a stayer. Was Xavier? He thought he wanted to be. Didn't a house and Lebowski prove he was a stayer? Wasn't that the whole purpose behind moving back to Cooper Springs? He'd needed a place to go after the disaster that was Arsen and a new direction. He wasn't just going to leave again once his Cooper Springs project was finished.

Xavier didn't think he would ever forget Lebowski's reaction when he spotted Xavier outside his kennel. His mom took a video of the whole thing; he'd check it out when they got home. Maybe even send it to Daisy. As Xavier had walked toward him, the floppy, long golden-haired retriever mix rose slowly to his feet, watching Xavier as if he couldn't believe his eyes. Lebowski's tail slowly moved back and forth, his gaze full of both hope and a question: *Is this really happening?*

Yes, Xavier thought. Because he *was* a stayer.

"I think they know when they get to go home," commented the shelter lady as she unlocked the gate and clipped the leash onto Lebowski's collar. "Come closer and say 'hi' again."

Kneeling, his knees protesting the cold cement floor, Xavier reached for Lebowski and was rewarded with a bundle of trembling blond dog in his lap and tentative doggy kisses that quickly covered Xavier's entire face.

"It's real, I promise," Xavier whispered against the dog's soft fur, tears blurring his vision.

Standing again, he swiped his eyes before he took the leash from the volunteer. He and Lebowski followed the volunteer and

Wanda to where Mop and Berkeley were patiently waiting, like they'd known Wanda was coming back. Or at least Mop had. Just in time, Xavier remembered to get out his phone and record the adoption.

First Mop trotted out from the kennel and allowed the volunteer to clip the leash on. She kept looking back over her shoulder, as if mentally telling the larger dog to hurry his ass up. Berkeley seemed unsure, and Xavier wondered if they'd tried to separate the two dogs in the past.

Wanda stepped into the kennel and snapped the second leash on Berkeley herself.

"Hey, sweetie, you're okay now, I've got you. Let's get the two of you home."

His mom's tender crooning triggered a slew of memories from when he was a kid. Bandaging skinned knees and elbows from crashing his bike—the "track" he and Forrest had constructed out of abandoned plywood and tires had not been the best idea they'd ever had. Her fierceness the first time he'd been called a derogatory name by kids he'd thought were friends.

He'd tried hiding his hurt, but somehow she'd figured out what happened. Then-principal Bert Adams had been a blustering fool at the meeting she'd insisted on having, claiming Xavier brought it on himself with his "outlandish" behavior. He'd retired a few years later and Xavier continued to wonder if his mom had a hand in that too.

Something seemed to click in Berkeley's head. He released a gleeful hound howl—bragging to everyone—and tugged on his leash, ready to put shelter life behind him.

"I wish I could take them all home," his mom commented over the cacophony resulting from other dogs barking their goodbyes.

On the drive home, his mom ended up sitting in the back seat between Mop and Berkeley, both of them vying for her lap. Lebowski rode up front next to Xavier, snapped into the harness, of course. The dog stared intently out the windshield as if trying to memorize the trip. Luckily, it wasn't a long drive because Berkeley sang her song of joy all the way to Cooper Springs.

"You're sure you'll be okay?" Xavier asked once they arrived at Wanda's house.

"Yes, sweetie," she assured him. "The shop is closed tomorrow, so we get to spend the whole day together, and Rufus promised he'd bring me lunch. Tonight, we'll just hang out and get to know each other better."

What with his brain being occupied obsessing over Vincent, Rufus Ferguson had slipped Xavier's mind. He opened his mouth to ask what was going on between them, but Wanda waved and walked away from his car, ready to be with her new family members. It wasn't any of his business, he supposed. If Rufus made his mom happy, then life was good.

Pulling to a stop in front of his house, Xavier couldn't stop himself from glancing across the street. Vincent's car wasn't in sight. The dashboard clock told him school wasn't out for another hour. And who knew, maybe there was tutoring or something he needed to do for Romy. Vincent had a lot of responsibilities riding on his shoulders. Maybe there wasn't space for Xavier. Maybe it was for the best.

Regardless, Wanda was right. Vincent wasn't like their dad, and if he really was "into" Vincent, he needed to work on his interpersonal communication. Maybe just his Vincent Barone communication.

Lebowski nosed at him impatiently, his tail flapping against the seat. Xavier grimaced, not from the cold dog nose but from the very real fact that, in all likelihood, he owed Vincent another apology.

He hoped having to apologize wouldn't become a habit. A

smile curved his lips; on the other hand, there'd been make-up sex after the last time.

Climbing out, he walked around the front of his car to the passenger side, opening the door to grab hold of Lebowski's leash before unclipping the seat harness. He didn't want to have to explain to the shelter, to his mother—to anyone—that he'd misplaced his new-to-him dog on the very first day. This wasn't like the hard-boiled egg experiment back in middle school where Xavier had forgotten his egg on the bus two hours after it was assigned to him. His brother had managed to hang on to his through the whole assignment and still teased Xavier about it.

Once they stepped inside, Xav toed off his shoes but kept Lebowski on his leash and walked him around the house, letting him take his time and smell everything he wanted. He was giving Lebowski a tour as if he was a human looking to buy a house. They finally arrived at his bedroom after an hour of extensive sniffing and exploration.

"This is my room," Xavier announced. "The bed looks nice, but keep your hairy mitts off it." The huge fluffy dog bed he'd bought lay on the floor next to Xavier's side of the bed. Was it odd he'd been single for almost a year and still slept on just one side? But it worked out because a mattress lasted twice as long. Right?

Maybe not if Vincent Barone shared his bed on a regular basis.

Nothing was permanent, he reminded himself, but maybe he was wrong this time. Like his mom had said, Vincent was a stayer.

Perhaps Wanda had a semi-valid point about being afraid potential partners would leave him. Then again, what if Vincent wasn't looking for a relationship anyway, and Xavier was going through all this irritating self-reflection for nothing?

He was exhausted from overthinking.

A knock on the front door caught both Xavier and Lebowski by surprise. Lebowski raced out of the bedroom and bounded down the stairs, the leash clattering behind him and his bark echoing throughout the house. Burglar alarm, check. Not that burglars knocked but it was another damn point for Vincent. Xavier felt better knowing his mom had a canine warning system.

Taking the stairs two at a time, he grabbed Lebowski's collar before he opened the door. Romy Barone stood on the other side, her eyes widening at the sight of the big ball of floof.

"Did you get a dog?" she exclaimed with a broad smile. She dropped to her knees in a way only the young can, letting the dog wiggle his hairy self against her and drag his tongue across her face.

"He?" She checked. "He's adorable! What's his name?"

"Lebowski. We got home from the shelter about an hour ago."

Romy rose to her feet, brushing tufts of hair off her clothing. The shelter people had warned Xavier that Lebowski might stress shed. At this rate, the dog was going to be bald by nightfall.

"Why don't you come in so I can take his leash off?"

The promised rain had held off until Xavier and Lebowski arrived home, but now it was dumping buckets and Romy was soaked through.

"Um, actually, my dad will have a cow if I"—raising her hands, she crooked her fingers—"'go into a stranger's house.' Not that I think you're a stranger, but he's super protective these days." She rolled her eyes in a manner that suggested Vincent was wildly overreacting.

He thought about the remains that had been found. If Romy were his daughter, Xav would probably have the same rules. He couldn't even be pissed at Vincent for this one.

"I forgot my keys at home this morning and I can't get in, and I tried calling him, but he hasn't picked up," she explained.

"He's at work?"

"I think he had a job after school. He said he had to go to Zenith. It sucks because I have homework I have to finish."

Zenith was in the unincorporated part of the county, only

about ten miles if there hadn't been a national forest in the way. It wasn't large enough to be a township and was a good forty-five-minute drive from Cooper Springs. If Vincent had left after school, he wouldn't be home before six.

Xavier glanced down at Lebowski, who was leaning against Romy's leg and staring adoringly up at her with his tongue lolling out.

"Hmm. I have an idea that is less likely to get us both in trouble with your dad, but does involve getting in my car for five whole minutes. Is that an equally terrible offense, or do you think we can get away with it just this once? If you and I both text him where you are and then send a proof-of-life selfie?"

He mentally patted himself on the back for letting his mom send him Vincent's cell phone number. Now he wouldn't have to stoop to asking Romy.

She wrinkled her nose. "Um, probably? But where?"

"My mom also adopted two dogs today. I bet she could use some help getting them used to her house. I'll order us pizzas and you can work on your homework while we're there. I don't know about you, but I haven't eaten lunch."

He had no idea about girls, but Xavier did recall Wanda complaining that he and Max ate like horses when they were having a growth spurt. Or, generally, anytime they were awake.

"Pizza sounds great," she said with a wide smile. "I love dogs! We can't have a pet. Dad says we're too busy and our house is too small."

"Okay. Good. Uh, do you mind holding onto Lebowski for a second?" No way was Xavier breaking the strange man's house rule. Technically, he and Vincent weren't strangers anymore, but Vincent obviously hadn't said anything to his daughter.

That was good. If things went sideways, they could pretend nothing had ever happened and ignore each other for the rest of their lives. And, ew, talking to kids about sex? Just no.

"Sure." Romy hiked her backpack higher on her shoulder as she reached for Lebowski's leash.

"Hold tight. I don't want him to escape."

He had to admit, though, it seemed like escape was the last thing on Lebowski's doggy mind. Back inside, he quickly called his mom from the landline to let her know he was coming over and Romy was tagging along, then he grabbed his cell phone and car keys.

"Let's go," he said, feeling pleased with himself and the solution he'd come up with as he beeped his car and opened the back door. Lebowski jumped in the back like a pro and Romy made herself comfortable in the front, reaching back to stroke Lebowski's head while Xavier navigated the roads.

FOURTEEN
VINCENT

Vincent stared down at his phone, his heart rate slowing after an initial burst of adrenaline. As soon as he'd rounded the bend that led into Cooper Springs and a random pocket of cell service, it had started buzzing. Thinking there was an emergency, he'd pulled over to check his messages, instantly worried something had happened to Romy.

Something *had* happened, that was certain. Lifting the phone, he peered at the selfie of Romy, Xavier, and Wanda. Wanda and Romy had wide smiles. Xavier looked either irritated or nervous, it was hard to tell from the picture. There was a second photo that looked like what he could remember of Wanda's backyard. Even though the picture was dark, he could still see a white mop-like dog wrestling with a larger golden dog while another dog monitored.

The text message from Romy read: **Pizza night at Wanda Stone's. Come over when you get home. Sorry, Dad. I forgot my keys and Xavier brought me here so you wouldn't accuse him of being a serial killer.**

Another text sent a minute later also from Romy read: **Xavier**

and Wanda are really nice, Dad, just so you know. Can we get a dog too?

Tucking his phone back into the cup holder between the front seats, Vincent groaned as he pulled the car back onto the road and headed directly to Wanda Stone's home. He didn't know how he felt about Xavier inserting himself into Romy's life. The last thing she needed was to get attached. And no way did they have time for a dog.

He sped—just a little—down the empty highway toward Cooper Springs, his car's headlights briefly lighting up the surrounding forest as he passed through it. Off to one side of the road, an animal's eyes glowed in reaction to the lights. The bulky profile told him it was a deer, not a Sasquatch. Pressing on the brake pedal, he slowed down. There was no rush. Romy was fine, safe and sound with Wanda Stone. And Xavier.

Xavier may not have had much experience with kids, but he'd known Vincent wasn't ready for Romy to hang out at his house. That might change soon enough but tonight it warmed Vincent's heart knowing Xavier had made a decision with him in mind. Hopefully he wasn't reading too much into what had happened the other night. Hopefully Xavier knew Vincent wasn't the kind of person who could have sex without feelings involved. Even if he wasn't quite ready to examine them.

Minutes later, he was passing Jack Watson's studio and home. Even in the dark, the totems and other carvings the Native American artist created and sold were easy to see. A carved raven, a unicorn—or maybe it was a narwhal. Sometimes it was hard to know with Jack. The road swept around another long curve and on the right were the Forest Service offices, locked up tight and dark except for the light on the front porch of the old log cabin building. These things were comforting, familiar. Vincent liked that his little town stayed mostly the same. Residents came and went, but the good things about Cooper Springs didn't change.

. . .

Romy opened the door for him. A bright smile lit up her face and from behind her came barking and the sound of dog claws scrabbling against tile, trying to gain purchase.

"Hurry." She grabbed his sleeve and tugged on it. "Get inside so the dogs don't get out."

Two dogs, the white moppy one and one that looked to be some kind of retriever, charged from the back of the house as Romy quickly shut the door behind him. They spotted Vincent and raced across the living room to investigate.

"The white one is Mop, and that's Lebowski," Romy said. "He's Xavier's."

Lebowski sniffed at his shoes while Mop lifted up onto her hind feet, her front paws resting on his thigh. Vincent patted the top of her head.

"Hi, Mop, nice to meet you."

"And that's Berkeley," Romy added.

A third dog had quietly entered the room and Vincent recognized it as the one watching the other two in the photo.

"Berkeley and Mop are a bonded pair."

"Come on into the kitchen!" Wanda called out. "Xavier is picking up the pizza, he'll be back in just a few minutes."

Vincent eyed his daughter. "Homework?"

"Daaad," his daughter groaned, sounding an awful lot like himself. "Wanda and Xavier invited us. We never do stuff like this. And I did do most of my homework already."

Watching her, Vincent wondered—not for the first time—if she'd inherited anything from her mother. Maybe the shape of her eyebrows? That tendency to corner him? Everything else, including the stubbornness and determination, came directly from him.

Relenting, he said, "Fine. This time." They both knew that, if the invitation was offered again, he would probably cave then, too.

Romy walked quickly toward the kitchen, almost, but not

quite, skipping. A small smile curved his lips. All he wanted in life was for his daughter to be healthy and happy.

Glancing up from chopping lettuce, Wanda greeted him with a smile as Vincent entered the kitchen. The dogs crowded in as well. Berkeley lay down under the table, his head on his paws, very watchful. Mop sat down next to him while Lebowski sat next to Romy, plopping his head in her lap.

"You have a lovely daughter, Vincent," Wanda said. "It's been a pleasure to have her here."

"I apologize for the imposition. I'm sure Romy won't forget her keys again."

"Oh, heavens, it was no imposition at all. In fact, she and I have come up with a plan." Wanda nodded toward Romy. "Do you want to run our idea by your dad? Or maybe, Vincent, you'd like something to drink first, before we overwhelm you with our plan for world domination? Water? Tea? I think there might be beer, and I always have wine for Xavier."

World domination sounded about right. He eyed Romy, who smiled innocently back as she stroked Lebowski's head, her notebook and a battered copy of Antigone splayed open page-side down in front of her. She'd at least been trying to work on her homework.

Shuddering at the sight of the classic, Vincent opened the cupboard where Wanda kept her drinking glasses. He'd hated being forced to read that book. It hadn't seemed relevant to his hormone-filled life. Why did school curriculums never change? It seemed a shame to ignore current literature.

"Water, but I'll get it. What's this plan?" Grabbing a glass, he moved to the sink to fill it while waiting for one of them to spill the idea they were both so excited about. Turning around so he could lean back against the counter, he took a drink of water and waited for an answer. Might as well get it over with.

"I'm going to need some help with my new friends," Wanda began, setting down the knife and facing him. "The shop is closed on Wednesdays and Thursdays right now—winter hours—so they'll be fine then, but, especially while they are settling in, I'd like to hire Romy to come over after school, when she can, and visit with them, take them out for a walk, that sort of thing. I would pay her, of course."

"Please, Dad?" Romy gave him her most beseeching look. "I could help with my drama fees and stuff!"

A serious downside of small-town life was the teen job market. There just weren't a lot of local jobs, even for adults. Working a few hours a week for Wanda Stone might work out well, certainly better than working at the sketchy Stop-N-Go on the edge of town.

"How many hours?"

Romy grinned. Wanda smiled, too, and filled him in on the plan, which seemed to involve a lot of homework time as well as dog-walking duties. Vincent forced himself to concentrate on the well-prepared sales pitch, but he was also listening for the front door to open again, realizing he was nervous about seeing Xavier. Monday night had been nothing short of incredible. Xavier Stone was smart, funny, sexy, and totally out of his league. Hopefully that last part wouldn't matter.

"So can I, Dad?" Romy's voice broke into his errant thoughts. Right, dog walking.

"Um, sure. Trial for now? We don't want your grades slipping and drama already takes a lot of your spare time. Speaking of which, do you know Daniella Brown? She's a sophomore too, moved to town maybe six weeks ago."

"I think I've seen her around. Why?"

"I don't think she's met anyone and seems kind of shy. I was wondering if you'd think about saying hi? Maybe invite her to sit with you, Vi, and Char once or twice during lunch. I think she's feeling a little lost."

Romy nodded. "Sure, I'll keep my eye out for her."

The sound of the front door opening reached his ears, and the butterflies Vincent had been trying to ignore began to drunkenly careen around in his stomach.

He could do this. He was a grown man. Luckily, the dogs jumped up and raced to the door to greet Xavier. Vincent's random embarrassment went unnoticed.

"Hey, everybody!" Xavier said as he strode into the kitchen, holding two pizza boxes high so the dogs wouldn't knock them out of his hands. "Sorry it took me so long." He shot an undecipherable glance toward Romy. "I ran into Critter."

Something in Xavier's tone had Vincent on high alert, and Wanda narrowed her eyes at her son.

Setting the pizza down on the counter and turning to face them, he said, "Critter, Mags, and Chief Dear recovered those remains, the ones that Jayden Harlow reported, this afternoon."

Wanda gasped and pressed a hand to her chest. "Oh, what a terrible job. But I'm glad whoever it is, is out of the elements now."

"Is it somebody we know?" Romy asked.

Vincent hoped not. Not that he wished death on a stranger. They wouldn't know anytime soon with how slowly the wheels of justice turned.

Xavier ran a hand through his hair. "I should've waited until we'd eaten, but I thought you'd all want to know. Critter said he and Mags weren't able to recognize the, um, person."

Vincent breathed a sigh of relief. Wanda sat at the table across from Romy, her eyebrows drawn together and looking a little pale. Vincent imagined he did too. Who'd lost their life out there? Vincent loved the forest he'd grown up with, but it wasn't a kind place for those who didn't know what they were doing. And sometimes it wasn't a kind place regardless.

"I guess they hadn't been able to get to it because of the rains until today," Xavier continued, "but someone reported Crook's

Trail was washed out up where it passes Elk Creek. Critter and Mags were planning on putting up warning signs, and Chief Dear and Lani went with them. Critter said that whoever it was had been there a while."

"What a tragedy," Wanda whispered. Berkeley sat up and leaned against her thigh, putting his head in Wanda's lap.

"What was someone doing up there alone?" Vincent wondered aloud. Crook's Trail was isolated, rugged, and damn steep. The reward was an incredible view of the region and bragging rights, but even Vincent—who felt he was a fairly accomplished outdoors person—wouldn't attempt it by himself.

Xavier shrugged, lifting the pizza box lids. "Who knows? Maybe it was a survivalist who thought they could beat the mountains. Anyway, I'm fu—er, *darn* hungry. Let's eat."

For a few minutes, they were quiet while they ate, probably all thinking about whoever had died alone in their forest. But soon enough the conversation started up again. Romy informed Xavier that Vincent had agreed to let her help with the dogs, which led to a discussion about whether Lebowski could join in the fun if Xavier was especially busy with clients. At the sound of his name, Lebowski's ears perked up and he moved around the table to plop his head into Xavier's lap, probably hoping for a bite of pizza.

Smiling, Xavier ran his hand across the top of Lebowski's head. "The dogs seem to be settling in really well. It's hard to believe it's only been a few hours."

"Lebowski knew when he saw you," Wanda said with a fond smile at her son. "And look at Mop and Berkeley. I probably shouldn't let them be under the table but I'm an old lady. I can do what I want."

Berkeley had slumped back down to the floor and curled up with Mop next to Wanda's feet.

"Dad," Romy said excitedly, "Xavier *has* to show you the video they took at the shelter. It's so cute!"

Obliging Romy's command, Xavier got his phone out so they

could all watch the video of Lebowski's adoption. Even Vincent had to admit—to himself only—that the scene was touching, and he kind of wished Xavier would look at him like that someday. As if he was completely amazed that someone wanted him.

Which wasn't awkward at all. The inconvenient emotions he'd been keeping at bay rushed back, along with all the butterflies. He stuffed a last bite of pizza into his mouth and stood up, taking his plate to the sink.

"Thanks for dinner, but we should get going."

Romy knew better than to protest, and in minutes, Vincent was behind the wheel, and they were heading home. Hopefully the butterflies wouldn't come along for the ride.

FIFTEEN
XAVIER

Across the street, a single overhead light illuminated Vincent's tiny excuse of a porch. It wasn't that late—Xavier had stayed at Wanda's house helping her clean up the kitchen and chatting for only another hour before making his excuses. He wondered if Vincent was working on that appraisal. And if Romy was also awake. If she was anything like Xavier when he'd been fifteen, then the answer was yes.

Was Vincent worried about the remains discovered on the mountain? Without a doubt, yes. Which was understandable, so was Xavier. Even though it sounded like the bones had been there for a while, the news was unsettling, and he'd been low-key anxious since the discovery.

Max had even called him yesterday, wanting to know what the hell was going on.

At dinner the night before, after Xavier had filled everyone in with what he'd learned from Critter, they'd avoided the grim subject and talked about almost anything else they could. Even the Friday night football game, which he'd somehow agreed to go to, even promising to meet Vincent there. What the fuck had he been thinking? He hadn't even gone to those when he'd been *in* high school. If Max found out, he'd never hear the end of it.

He'd never had the chance to pull Vincent aside and check if he was okay with what had happened between them the other night. Not that his mother's house was the time or place, but he wasn't sure if there'd ever really be a time or place—Xavier had a client coming to town the next day and Vincent was busy too.

Of course, he'd needed to be home when Romy woke up; how stupid of Xavier to jump to the conclusion that Vincent was ashamed, or that he regretted what they'd done. If anything, he was probably still processing what had happened between them.

Right?

Yes.

When Xavier had first walked back into Wanda's house with the pizzas, he'd sensed Vincent was feeling awkward, like he wasn't sure how to act. Which meant they needed to talk and not just spin their wheels, imagining what the other was thinking. Damn his mother for being right. Again. Not that he was going to tell her that.

Lebowski's cold nose bumped against his neck, making him jump and reminding him he couldn't just sit in his car all night and obsess about his hot, kind, responsible neighbor. He had his own commitments.

"Fine, let's go inside."

An hour later, Lebowski had gobbled his kibble and been let out into the yard for five minutes to sniff and pee. Xavier was showered, had donned his favorite pair of sleep pants, and was under the covers, ready to aim the remote at his TV and tune out for a little while.

Something cold bumped his hand, and he looked down. Lebowski's head was resting on the edge of the bed. He was literally giving him puppy-dog eyes.

Xavier shook his head. "I shouldn't let you on the bed. That's how bad habits start."

Lebowski released the tiniest, most pathetic sigh Xavier had ever heard in his life and added a miniscule tail twitch. Surely one time wouldn't count? This was Lebowski's first night in his new home, after all.

"Fine, you can get up here, but just this once."

Lies pet owners tell themselves and other stories.

He patted the mattress and Lebowski didn't hesitate. Jumping up, he turned three times and lay down at the end of the bed, sighing again, but this time with pleasure.

"I am a sucker and have no one to blame but myself," Xavier informed the dog and was rewarded with a twitch of his floofy tail.

Looking away from the dog, Xavier glanced at his phone sitting on the side table.

To text Vincent? Or not to text Vincent? That was the question.

Picking it up, Xavier typed: **Hi, it's Xavier. My mom gave me your number.**

Was this middle school? Fuck. He stared at the screen long enough that it went dark. His mom had given him the number, but... really? Did he want to lead with his *mother*?

"Christ, we've had sex, for crying out loud." He pressed Send anyway. Who knew if Vincent was still awake? Or if his phone was powered up? Maybe he didn't text—the spotty cell service meant it wasn't a habit people got into around town even if they did have their phones on home wi-fi.

There, he'd done it. He moved to set the phone back down, but it vibrated in his hand.

Vincent: I'm glad you texted. I've been so busy I haven't seen you. Sorry about leaving the other night. I wanted to be home when Romy woke up.

Xavier: After sulking (I apologize) I realized that was probably why you had to go home.

Vincent: In my defense you were sound asleep.

Xavier: Best night of "sleep" I've had in years.

Vincent: ... ... really?

Xavier: Yes, really.

Vincent: I'm just surprised. It's not like I have much experience.

Xavier: Believe me, it was incredible.

He hesitated, his fingers hovering over his screen.

and we could do it again if you want more practice.

Vincent: ... ...

Dammit, did that sound like a booty call? Vincent was not booty-call material. Although Xavier wasn't sure how to label him.

Xavier: Believe it not, I think I like you for more than just your body. We could try going on a

Did he want to use the word date? No, he did not. He deleted the "a" and instead typed: to the pub for a drink?

Was that too much? Too soon? How much second-guessing could he manage in forty seconds? A lot.

Vincent: You type really fast. My fat fingers are not good at this. Like a date? Don't want to assume.

Shutting his eyes for a moment as his heart started racing, Xavier breathed in a calming breath. Lebowski twitched against his feet, smiling in his sleep.

Xavier: Yes, like a date. Although I'm not sure if the Donkey counts.

Vincent: I'd like that. Should have a talk with Romy first. Maybe after the football game? Romy will probably stay over with one of her friends.

Xavier stared at the words on the screen. A shiver ran through him. and goose bumps formed on his arms.

Vincent wasn't out.

But he was willing to out himself just for a drink with Xavier at their local pub. The pub where all the town gossips hung out. Xavier's heart skipped a beat before righting itself.

Xavier: Are you sure? Townies talk.

Vincent: Liam saw me leaving your house, pretty sure most of the town already knows. By Friday, people will be asking when I'm going to make an honest man of you.

With fingers that only trembled slightly, Xavier typed back, **Okay, Friday after the game.**

It was a good thing Vincent couldn't see him right now. His skin was clammy and cold and he wondered if he was going to throw up. Did he want Vincent to make an honest man of him?

Xavier was afraid he did.

Until Vincent, dating in Cooper Springs had been a hard no-fly zone. He'd joked with Max and his mom about the dating pool being limited to just three men and one of them was himself. But the real truth was, the last *date* Xavier'd had in town had been over twenty years ago and had ended with him getting four stitches over his eyebrow. His supposed date had instead invited his asshole friends along and they'd jumped him. Even though his small hometown had changed since then, his stomach still roiled at the betrayal.

Lebowski lifted his head, blinking at him. Could he sense Xavier's inner turmoil? He oozed closer to Xavier and ended up pressed against his side.

"Thanks, buddy, I needed that."

Vincent: Friday, be there or be square.

God, he was so *there*.

Over the next couple of days, the news about the discovery on Crook's Trail was the topic on everyone else's mind around town —except for Xavier's—meaning he couldn't avoid hearing every possible theory and all the details Chief Dear wasn't able to keep secret.

He'd learned from his mom who'd heard it from Rufus that, when they'd hiked in to bring the remains down, they'd found some scattered clothing but no identification. The remains did not appear to be those of a hiker or camper. Possibly the person could have stripped their clothing off if they'd had hypothermia, but Critter had said they'd found flip-flops near the remains.

No one in their right mind would hike Crook's in flip-flops.

Xavier was certain these details weren't supposed to be as widely known as they were. But a small town was not a place for secrets—unless you were an outsider and then all bets were off. The flapping lips must have made this kind of investigation difficult for Andre Dear and the rest of the CSPD.

In order not to obsess over the *date* with Vincent on Friday, Xavier kept himself busy. He met with the mayor, sharing his idea for a winter art festival—he'd ease into the chainsaw part later—and throwing his support, and sponsorship, behind Summer Beach Shakespeare. The mayor hinted she'd look into the permitting for the summer festival but clearly Xavier needed to work harder to sell her on the winter art fest.

Thursday, he spent the day with a client who he hoped to sell on his Cooper Springs rejuvenation project. Tim Dennis was an old friend from his college days who had money to burn and, in his own words, wanted to "use it for good and not evil."

Xavier always enjoyed Tim's company—he was easygoing and had a wicked sense of humor. He was grateful Arsen hadn't driven Tim away.

Gripping the BMW's steering wheel, Xavier deftly navigated a series of deep, sweeping curves that led south from the edge of Olympic National Park toward the junction leading to Cooper Springs. Where they were now, the forest came right up against the roadway, casting wonky afternoon shadows that tricked the eye. It was easy for Xavier to imagine sneaky forest creatures watching them pass by.

"It's gorgeous out here. In a sort of dark and mysterious way. Different from Piedras Island," his passenger said, echoing his thoughts.

"What? Oh, yeah." Xavier nodded. "It is. There's a reason we have our own Bigfoot Society and any number of UFO hunters living out here."

"Surely there's room for growth? How many UFO hunters can one community support?" Tim asked.

Initially, Xavier had called Tim about some undeveloped land that had recently come on the market. After showing him the parcel, which Tim seemed only mildly excited about—and wasn't the reason why he'd lured his friend to Cooper Springs anyway— Xavier had spent the rest of Thursday afternoon driving him around the community, upselling the county's potential for growth. He had a plan and needed Tim to see what he saw before unfurling it.

"You'd be surprised how many believers we have. But, yes, positive growth is what we need. Not the kind that cuts trees down, kills wildlife, and makes everyone mad," Xavier joked.

Or people disappearing.

"That set of cabins you just sold is going to bring new folks to town. What you guys need now is branding for the tourists. Use those UFOs and the Sasquatch sightings to bring in folks who like quirky stuff."

Xavier mentally high-fived himself. Tim was intrigued.

"This isn't branding, but what do you think about a weekend with Shakespeare on the beach combined—or not—with a chainsaw art competition?" Xavier hadn't forgotten his moment of brilliance. The idea had been rolling around in his head since mentioning it to Magnus and Forrest. "Aiming for both the arty types and the flannel crowd."

"Are you serious?" Tim asked, laughing.

"As a heart attack. There needs to be something more than rustic cabins to draw visitors. And honestly, it may take the buyer a while to get them up and going."

"Huh, true. Well, maybe not plays and chainsaws on the same weekend because I can tell you right now, I'd want to go to both. The Shakespeare would have to be in August, right? Because of the weather? Maybe have the chainsaw art competition in March or April? Could it be done in tents?"

Xavier thought about Liam's front yard and the tent he had set up as a studio.

"Why not?" Why couldn't they set up tents for the competitors? "My neighbor has a pretty cool setup in his front yard. I bet we could do something like that."

Now they were passing through Zenith, a mining town back in the day, but now just a cluster of grubby, run-down buildings huddled close to the road. Maybe Xavier had a case of rose-colored glasses, but he swore he could visualize the changes just a small investment would bring to the community. The area was rife with micro-communities needing micro-funding. An espresso stand at the four-way stop, a trinket shop on the corner. Xavier just needed to figure out how to get the funding and the needy together. *This* was why he'd moved back to the area.

That and the need for a fresh start. If starting fresh was moving back to his economically challenged hometown, then he'd succeeded. But his plans were bigger than that. He wanted to do something big for Cooper Springs and he thought Tim Dennis could help.

Tim's head turned, looking one way and then the other at the scattered homes set away from the road, the overgrown pastures, and the abandoned fruit tree orchards. "Are those apple trees?"

Xavier nodded. "Yep, believe it or not, we can grow apples out here. No cherries, it's too cold and damp, but plenty of apples and pears."

"That's cool. Is anyone actively growing them now? To sell?"

"Not really, but I'm working on it."

This was the real reason he'd called Tim. The heart of the deal.

"What does that mean? I sense a plan."

Xavier wanted to do a fist pump, but he resisted. Tim was hooked.

"A local guy I grew up with owns some acreage north of town, we drove past it when we looked at that first property. He has an acre, maybe more, of apple trees. They're old, planted in the 1950s. But back in the day they were the pride of Cooper Springs —along with saltwater taffy and kite flying. I've been trying to convince him to start a boutique cidery."

"What's stopping him?"

"Levi is worried about the money, of course, and he keeps pointing out that he can't keep a house plant alive. *I* keep pointing out that the trees have managed fine for over seventy years, so I don't think that's a problem. But he will need to learn the cider business."

"I suppose it isn't coincidence that you lured me out here?" Tim chuckled. "Seeing as I do know how to make cider and run a cidery as well."

While Xavier had been pursuing his still unused English degree, Tim had gotten a degree in business and a certificate in craft brewing. His twenty-year career as both brewer and businessman was something Xavier envied. If anyone Xavier knew could help Levi start a cidery, it was Tim.

"Nope," he said with a grin. "You need a new project, a challenging one."

Tim sighed, but Xavier noticed he didn't argue.

Pulling up at the single stop sign in Zenith—Cooper Springs at least had two stop signs and one stop light—he spotted a boy who looked to be around thirteen or fourteen, waiting for them to pass by. Xavier waved for him to cross, and he shot them a suspicious glower before stepping into the road.

As he passed in front of his car, Xavier thought the kid looked familiar, but he couldn't place him. Only two of his friends had kids and they were both girls. Glancing in the rearview mirror, Xavier watched the kid disappear into the woods on the other side of the road. What was he doing, hiking? Maybe buying drugs from some creep that hung out there? It was too late and close to dark and too cold for hiking.

Another couple miles closer to Cooper Springs it hit him that the teen might have been Jayden Harlow, the kid who'd found the first set of remains. Xavier wondered whatever happened to Corey Harlow. In high school, Corey had always said he was leaving Cooper Springs in the dust and never coming back—but obviously he hadn't. They hadn't exactly been friends back then, but they'd spent time in detention together. If Xavier wanted the truth, he'd have to ask his mom; for the rumor and hearsay, he'd check in with Magnus.

On the outskirts of town, they hit traffic. Frowning, Xavier braked, wondering what the hell was going on.

"Damn, I hope there's not an accident."

"I don't see any flashing lights ahead," Tim said.

Inching north up the roadway, they eventually arrived at the epicenter of the jam—CSPD headquarters, a low-slung, gray, single-story brick building built in the fifties that could just as easily be mistaken for a post office. Chief Dear stood on the front steps, facing several reporters who were aggressively shoving mics toward his face.

"What's that all about?" Tim asked.

"Nothing good," Xavier said glumly. "A week or so ago, a kid found human bones on one of the trails. From what I've heard, they'd probably been there awhile. But they could be a girl who went missing last summer, hopefully not. That's the only reason I can think of for the news to be interested in our little town. Next time reporters are here, it will be to cover chainsaw art and beach Shakespeare."

Ahead of them, Lani Cooper stood on the center line waving cars past the station, the piercing call of her police whistle sounding when drivers slowed down too much. Xavier did not make that mistake.

"Angela Wiggen," said Tim out of the blue.

Xavier risked a glance at his passenger. "Yes, how did you know?"

"She's on a couple of billboards in Aberdeen."

Right.

"That's right, I'd forgotten about that. But, yes, I'm hoping it isn't her."

The cars ahead of them sped up, and so did Xavier.

Not even a minute later, Xavier pulled into the parking lot in front of his office.

"Want to grab a drink?" Tim asked.

Turning off the engine, Xavier glanced at his passenger. If luck was on their side, he and Tim—a stranger from out of town— could have a couple beers and no one would speculate. He didn't need some weird gossip getting back to Vincent.

"I could use a drink."

Tim laughed as he pushed his door open. "You don't sound very sure."

"A glass of wine sounds good. Just so you know, gossip is this town's favorite pastime and any gossip worth their salt hangs out at the Donkey."

"I can handle a little gossip if you can."

. . .

The pub was about half full, and Xavier recognized everyone inside. Every single lip flapper who called Cooper Springs home was present. Magnus was behind the counter, pouring beers for Liam and Forrest, while Rufus occupied his spot at the end of the bar, likely rehashing the only gossip in town right now—the remains. Magnus's eyes widened when he spotted Xavier and Tim before his gaze moved to the seating area. Xavier followed his line of sight and saw that Vincent was sitting alone in one of the booths.

From Magnus's reaction, Xavier knew he hadn't been wrong about the entire town knowing that he and Vincent were circling around each other. *Thank you, Liam.* Sucking in a breath and internally rolling his eyes, Xavier wound his way between the tables toward Vincent, hoping Tim didn't mind meeting someone new.

"Hey," he said.

Vincent had been so focused on his laptop, he must not have noticed Xavier's and Tim's arrival.

Blinking, he stared up at them. "Oh, hi."

"Can we join you, or are you working?"

"I'm working, but I don't want to so, please, have a seat." He waved at the other side of the booth.

Xavier slid onto the bench seat across from Vincent.

"Vincent, this is Tim Dennis. He's an old friend from college. We spent the day driving around the countryside. Tim, Vincent lives across the street from me."

They shook hands, and Tim sat down next to Xavier. Closing his laptop, Vincent pushed it to one side.

"School work or appraisal work?" Xavier asked him.

"Finishing an appraisal. Sydney needs it for a job in Elma ASAP. Normally I can do a little work on them while I'm at school, but I had to be on top of it today." He rolled his eyes. "It's bad enough Halloween is coming up. That, and with the remains being found, not one of them was working on their projects."

"Ah, Halloween. I forgot that was coming up. I suppose that

explains all the pumpkins and vampires in people's yards. Vincent teaches shop at the local high school," Xavier explained to Tim.

"Do you get hazard pay for that?" Tim asked.

Vincent snorted. "I wish."

Magnus approached the booth to take their order. "What are you drinking tonight?" He growled, shooting Xavier a frosty glance that had Xavier mentally rolling his eyes again.

"A glass of white wine, thanks. Magnus, this is an old *friend* from college, Tim Dennis."

"Magnus Ferguson, Publican," Magnus grunted. "What can I pour you?"

"Do you have Guinness?" asked Tim.

Tim's request defrosted Magnus a tad more. "Of course, we have Guinness. Pint or pint?"

Tim chuckled. "I guess I'll have a pint."

"Good choice."

"Vincent?"

"I'll have one of those IPAs you were telling me about."

"Coming up," Magnus said, sketching a bow before turning and striding back to the taps.

"What crawled into his cornflakes?" Xavier muttered, knowing exactly what Magnus was thinking.

"I dunno." Vincent frowned too. "He was fine when I got here. Maybe his dad is giving him a hard time."

While Rufus lived to rib his son, Xavier did not think that was the issue.

"I have a good idea what he's pissed about," Xavier said. "And while I appreciate Magnus's loyalty, Tim really is just a friend."

Vincent's gaze flicked to the bar where Liam and Forrest still occupied two barstools. Forrest was talking, his hands going everywhere, while Liam listened and drank his beer.

He winced. "Oh, right. Shoot."

Tim glanced back and forth between them, but Xavier wasn't

going to out Vincent without permission. Vincent met his gaze, winked, and nodded his okay.

"Vincent and I"—Xavier began wishing he had that glass of wine already—"are, have, ugh." Sweat broke out on his forehead. "We're seeing each other." There he'd done it. And remarkably, his world was the same.

"Yep," Vincent agreed, "and it seems Magnus is feeling protective of me—which is funny in its own way. Until recently, as far as anyone in town knew, I was just a boring shop teacher and single dad, known for sticking to the rules. Xavier has me breaking a few rules, but I'm still a boring shop teacher and single dad."

"And still a stickler for most of the rules." Xavier nudged Vincent's ankle with his foot.

Vincent returned the tap as he leaned back against the back of the booth. "Yep, and proud of it."

Magnus returned with their drinks and set them on the table.

Tim lifted his Guinness. "To breaking the rules!"

They clinked their glasses together and each of them took a sip. Xavier met Vincent's amused gaze. Who could have predicted he'd be toasting Vincent Barone breaking rules? And that the "rule" was him.

SIXTEEN

VINCENT

"It was nice to meet you, Tim," Vincent said a pint later and after they'd vacated the booth to head out to the parking lot. Big surprise, the rain had started up again. "See you tomorrow, Xavier. I hope you haven't forgotten about the football game."

Xavier groaned and bumped Vincent's shoulder. "Do I have to go? Can't we just meet at the Donkey after the game is over?"

Tim snorted. "Xavier's going to a football game? I feel like there's an almost-twenty-year-old bet I might be winning."

Vincent shook his head. "No can do. Romy is expecting you to be there. Not that we'll see her."

"Fine," Xavier groused. "I'll be there."

"It must be serious if you convinced Xavier to go to a game," Tim commented. "He refused to set foot in the stadium when we were in college."

"Football was always better enjoyed behind the stands, or underneath," Xavier said haughtily. "I'm a fan of guys in tight pants, but they were all look and no touch."

Ignoring that comment, Vincent beeped his car and walked around to the driver's side. "See you later. I need to get home and see what Romy is up to."

He got behind the wheel, and Xavier and Tim started walking toward Xavier's office where they'd left their cars. The drive home was quick—Cooper Springs after dark in October was not a happening place—except on game nights. But, after listening to Xavier and Tim brainstorm ideas that might bring more business to town, Vincent thought things could be changing.

And surely Xavier had been kidding when he mentioned an extreme chainsaw competition? Vincent shuddered, imagining fingers and other bits flying off people at alarming rates.

Vincent wanted to wait for Xavier to get home so they could talk, but he needed to get inside his own house and check in with his teenaged daughter. Romance as a single father was a bit harder than if he'd been on his own. Romy was a good kid, but good kids needed attention too. After all the recent news, he wanted to hug her tightly and tell her how much he loved her, how important she was to him.

He also needed to talk to her about him and Xavier. Even if she thought she already knew, Vincent had to be open about it with her. Romy came first. Although he'd rather have an in-person interview with the IRS.

"Hi, Dad," Romy greeted him as he came through the door. She was curled up on their couch, with what appeared to be her homework sitting open on her lap. "I thought you'd be home before now."

"Why? Did you forget your key again?"

He was going to make her start wearing her keys on a chain around her neck if she kept forgetting them.

"No," she scoffed, "I didn't forget my key. Jeez, you're soaking. What were you doing?"

"I stopped in at the Donkey and ran into Xavier and a friend of his." Peeling his coat off, he hung it on the hooks mounted on the back of the door. Hesitating, he scraped a hand through his damp hair, a nervous tic of his. Nervous or not, they needed to have a conversation.

But he could put it off until he dried off a bit.

Toeing his shoes off, he left them by the door and headed to his bedroom to grab a change of socks from the drawer and sweats and a long-sleeved t-shirt from his closet.

He didn't want to share his dating life with Romy, but he wanted to go out in public with Xavier—as more than a friend—and Romy deserved to know first. Of course, that horse had left the barn, but he still owed her the conversation. Halting, with his shirt halfway over his head, he suddenly thought, what if people in town started saying crappy things? What if—nope, he couldn't go there. The important person in all this was his daughter. He finished pulling his shirt down and then his sweater, but he took the socks with him back out to the living room where he plopped on the other end of the couch.

Instead of looking at Romy, he focused on pulling the socks on over his feet.

"I have something I want to talk to you about," Vincent said to one thick wool sock as he dragged it over his foot.

"Am I in trouble?" Romy asked. "I took the trash out when I got home."

"No, you're not in trouble. I, uh, just wanted you to know that Xavier and I are meeting for a drink at the Donkey after the game tomorrow. I didn't want you to hear it through the rumor mill."

"A drink as in a date?"

Vincent nodded, still not looking at her. "As in a date."

"Sqeee!" Jumping up off the couch, Romy spun in a gleeful circle. "I knew it!"

He eyed his daughter. "What do you think you knew?"

"I *knew* you liked him. You always complain about people and then like them. It's like your superpower."

"It is not."

"Is too."

He stopped himself from saying, "is not" again because that was just proving Romy's point.

"Besides, you were acting funny the other day when we were at Wanda's." She made weird googly eyes at him.

Automatically, Vincent opened his mouth to correct her to "Ms. Stone" but remembered that Wanda had requested Romy call her by her first name.

"I wasn't acting funny," he lied. "I'd had to rush back from work and found out you were at Wanda's and was flustered."

"Is that what they called it back when the dinosaurs roamed the earth, flustered?" Romy cackled at her own joke as she resumed her position on the couch.

Vincent was not amused. Not that amused.

"Getting back to the subject at hand. Are you okay with me and Xavier seeing each other? I can't predict the future, we could end up hating each other. But if we do, uh, date, I knew you'd hear about it and wanted to make sure it's okay with you."

What if this didn't go anywhere and Romy had to deal with the town gossips? The town gossips, he reminded himself, seemed to be rooting for him. But just maybe he was jumping into this thing with Xavier too soon? The last thing he wanted to happen was Romy experiencing blowback because he'd decided his neighbor was hot.

"I think it's great, Dad." Romy assured him. "I like Xavier a lot, he's funny and doesn't talk down to me. I like his mom too."

"So, just to recap, you're okay with me seeing where this goes? And if it doesn't go anywhere, that's okay too? And if people say bad things around school?"

"Haters gonna hate, Dad. But my friends think you're pretty cool. Maybe a few will be jerks, but they live sad, lonely lives and need to get a hobby. As long as I can still take care of Berkeley and Mop. And Lebowski, when Xavier needs help."

How was his kid so smart? Vincent mostly felt like he was

feeling around in the dark. But, he admitted, her brains clearly did not come from Carly.

Her comment about Xavier replayed in his head. "When did he turn from Mr. Stone to Xavier?"

"When we hung out at his mom's house. Wanda said it was too weird calling them Mr. Stone and Mr. Stone's mom."

Vincent chuckled, imagining Wanda Stone putting her foot down. "Good. That's good."

Then Romy brought up the other thing everyone in town was talking about. The remains.

"Everybody's talking about what Critter and Mags found on Crook's Trail. Do you think it's the girl?"

He *hated* that no one needed to say her name to know who they were referring to. She wasn't just a girl, she was a daughter, maybe a sister, somebody's best friend. And she'd been missing for three months. Vanished. Gone. No trace.

"I haven't heard anything one way or the other. I think it can take a while to, um, identify remains. And it's not as if we have a huge police department. There's no forensics team. Cooper Springs is not nearly big enough for that kind of thing."

"That's not right," Romy said fiercely. "I'm going to study criminology, and one thing I'll do is fight for more funding for rural police stations. It's not right that people go missing or whatever and there's no one to care what happened to them."

Yep, her brains definitely did not come from Carly. Romy had a compassionate streak a mile wide. Vincent worried that part of her personality might bring her pain in the future, but he wouldn't want her to lose it.

"And what if she asked for help and no one did anything? It's not right! What if she asked for help and people just turned their backs on her?!"

"People do care, but no, it's not right," Vincent agreed. "All we can do is try to change the future. Years ago, the high school used to have what they called a 'safe space' after-school program, but it ended when funding was cut. Maybe we should talk to Principal Robinson about seeing if there's a way to start something like that up again?"

If nothing else, he'd stay after school when he could and hang out with kids who needed an adult, someone to listen to them. It wouldn't solve everything, but he'd feel like he was doing something.

"That would only help kids in our community."

"We have to start somewhere," he said. "Hopefully, it's not her. Hopefully Angela Wiggen is somewhere safe." But they both knew, wherever Angela was, she probably wasn't coming back. Turning to face Romy, he asked another question that was burning a hole in his gut. "You'd talk to me if you were unhappy? No matter what? Or another adult you trust." He hoped Romy trusted him enough to come to him, but if talking to someone else meant she stayed safe, he'd have to accept that.

"Yes, Dad."

Sensing he needed reassurance, she stood up again, stepped around the coffee table, and bent down to wrap her arms around him. He squeezed his daughter back as tight as he dared before releasing her and slumping against the cushions again.

"Thanks, kiddo, I needed that."

Romy scowled. "Blargh, *kiddo*."

"Look, it could be worse. I could call you *my little sweet pumpkin* or something. Um, I'm just going to head over and check in with Xavier, let him know I talked to you, okay? Lock the door after me."

"Yes, Dad, it's fine and I'll be sure to lock the door. Don't stay up past your bedtime!" She tossed him a knowing smirk.

He ignored her insinuation. He just couldn't let himself go there where his own kid was concerned. "Don't worry, I have work to finish tonight. Especially if you want that new tool set you've been pestering me about."

"Thanks, Dad. Once I start taking care of the dogs regularly,

I'll be able to help out with the money I earn. And I do want to talk to Principal Robinson."

The earnest expression on her face made Vincent want to hug her again, but he figured he'd already used up his hug token for the day.

"Okay, let's make a plan. You should put your earnings in savings. It's not like I've been able to put much aside for college. Life won't be getting cheaper anytime soon. We can talk more about it later."

Drama. Football games. Maybe—probably— a car in her future. Romy was going to need her own money.

"Okay, Dad."

Crossing to the front window, he peeked outside and noted the rain had let up a bit. Backlit by the block's single streetlight, a light mist drifted down. It almost looked like snow, but it wasn't that cold and it rarely snowed on the coast. Leaving his coat hanging on the door, he shoved his feet into his loafers. A ratty sweatshirt Romy had given him for his thirty-fifth birthday, *World's Best Dad* emblazoned across the chest, hung next to his coat. Grabbing the sweatshirt, he pulled it on and twisted the door handle.

"See you in a bit," he said as he pulled the door shut.

"Don't hurry on my account!" Romy shouted after him.

Vincent kept moving, pretending he hadn't heard a word.

Lebowski let out a sharp bark as Vincent jogged up the porch stairs of Xavier's house. The door opened almost immediately, and Xavier greeted him with a pleased smile creasing his handsome face. Lebowski lunged forward to say hello, but Xavier had a tight grip on his collar.

"Hey, come on in. I wasn't expecting to see you until game time tomorrow."

Xavier had changed clothes too. Instead of his real estate

agent casual, he now had on a well-worn pair of blue jeans that rode low enough on his hips Vincent could see a sliver of skin and also a black Henley with the sleeves pushed up over his toned forearms. And bare feet. Bare feet were almost as sexy as a hairy chest. Not that he was noticing.

Flustered by how quickly his thoughts headed south, Vincent toed off his loafers, at the same time realizing he was dressed in dad gear. There was nothing remotely sexy about loafers, sweats, and an ancient sweatshirt. Not that he had plans—or the time—for any sort of seduction tonight, did he?

No. No, he did not.

"Game time," Vincent repeated Xavier's words, trying to instill a bit of control over the conversation. Although he suspected that was a lost cause. "Are you practicing sporty terminology for the game tomorrow?"

"Hey," Xavier protested. He let go of Lebowski and the dog rushed over to sniff Vincent. "I know sports stuff."

Lebowski decided Vincent was not a dangerous intruder and wandered into the living room where he plopped down on the area rug.

"Uh-huh, like what?"

Xavier waggled his stupidly sexy eyebrows. "Is this a pop quiz, Mr. Barone?" Locking the door, he stepped closer to Vincent. Close enough Vincent could smell Xavier's aftershave and the scent of his clothes, fresh out of the dryer. "I might need to stay after school, get some one-on-one tutoring. I do know all about man-on-man coverage though."

"As much as the idea of a private session is... enticing"—so damn enticing Vincent to had force himself to keep speaking—"can I take a rain check? I just wanted to let you know I talked to Romy about uh, us, and"—his cheeks were molten hot—"she's on board."

Lordy, he felt like a teenager courting for the first time. But his reward was Xavier's expression, a mix of pleasure and surprise. As if he hadn't really expected Vincent to follow through.

"She's a smart kid." Inching closer to Vincent, Xavier hooked one finger into the waistband of Vincent's Super-Sexy Sweats, sending a delicious shiver down his spine. "Come here, you at least deserve a kiss."

As if Vincent was going to deny himself a kiss.

Xavier leaned in and pressed his lips against Vincent's. He knew he shouldn't stay, but tasting Xavier was his new favorite thing, Romy would be okay. She'd told him not to hurry. Without consciously thinking about what it would lead to, his lips parted so he could welcome Xavier inside. Xavier's tongue flicked against his, teasing and taunting. Vincent's hands rose, cupping Xavier's rough cheeks, keeping him in place to better taste him. His dick rose too. Vincent couldn't deny he wanted Xavier any way he could get him, even if it meant a hasty make-out session in Xavier's foyer.

Groaning, Xavier shoved Vincent backward, until only the wall behind him kept him upright. There was no way Xavier would miss his erection and Vincent didn't want him to. The reason why they shouldn't do this tonight, right now—forgotten. All that mattered right now was touching, feeling, tasting. Years of not having anyone, of not even caring that he didn't have anyone, fell away, leaving need in their place. Need for Xavier Stone, the one man who made Vincent break his own rules.

"You seem to have an extra-credit assignment for me, Mr. Barone," Xavier whispered in Vincent's ear as one hand dropped downward. He cupped Vincent's package, driving him closer to an edge he wanted to leap off of. "I *love* extra credit."

His balls twitched and pulsed, and Vincent thrust into Xavier's grip, needing more. The deep groan that echoed up the stairwell was his, at least he thought so.

"Are you sure you can't stay?" Xavier stared into his eyes. His tongue darted out to wet his lips—or to tease Vincent even further—and his fingers were hooked into Vincent's waistband again.

"No," Vincent rasped, "I'm not sure about anything."

Still staring into his eyes, Xavier began to push down the sweats and the plain boxers Vincent wore underneath.

"God, Vincent, you are something else. Something good, something amazing. Something I'm not sure I deserve. But" — he shot Vincent an absolutely wicked smile—"I'm going to take it."

Vincent wanted to take what the universe was offering them too, he wanted to grab it with both hands and run. He'd been alone for so long it had become habit to him. And often a cloak that protected him from the world. He was Vincent Barone: never hasty, never made rash decisions, always reasonable.

"Xavier," Vincent drew his name out, the last pathetic fluttering vestiges of his resolve fading to nothing as the man in question dropped to his knees in front of him.

"It's homework time, Mr. Barone."

If the wall hadn't been holding him up, Vincent would've fallen. Hell, with Xavier's mouth on him and around him, Vincent felt the ground move under his feet anyway. His ugly pants were down around his ankles and Xavier Stone was on his knees with Vincent's cock in his mouth, doing things that made thinking impossible. No fantasy came close to the real thing, to the real Xavier Stone.

Xavier was watching him through his thick lashes, his lips pulled taut because Vincent wasn't small. Vincent tried to keep his eyes open, but the sensation, the pure pleasure was too much, and he had to lean his head back and shut his eyes, letting himself feel and surf the tsunami he was riding—or it was riding him.

He meant to warn Xavier when his balls tightened and the spark at the base of his spine blazed, alerting him he was about to come. But his brain was sluggish and he had no words anyway.

Instead, he let go of the wall and dove his fingers into Xavier's hair, not pulling but *possessing*.

"Damn," he whispered roughly as he flew over that edge, shooting come down Xavier's throat. Letting his hands fall back to his side, Vincent managed to crack his eyes open while his heart pounded against his ribs and he tried to get his breath back.

With a smug expression on his face, Xavier rose to his feet, wiping his mouth with the back of his hand.

"Do I get full marks?"

Vincent let his own lascivious smile curve his lips. "Full marks. Maybe even more than full marks."

Xavier leaned against him. Even with those sinful jeans between them, the heat of his erection was scalding.

"So, extra-extra credit? That was okay? Are you mad I ravished you in the front hall?"

"Believe me, I am not mad. I think I like being ravished. It's your turn now," Vincent said. He wasn't the kind of man to leave someone hanging. Even though they were new, still working through what this was between them, he would give as equally as he'd received.

Adjusting his stance, Vincent snaked one hand into Xavier's pants, surprised when he didn't encounter anything as he wrapped his fingers around him.

"You're not wearing any underwear. God," he groaned, "now every time I see you, I'm going to wonder what you have on under your clothing."

He was rewarded with the huff of a laugh and a moan of pleasure. Xavier's cock fit in his hand perfectly. Unyielding beneath the soft, almost silky skin protecting it. Vincent let out a grunt of frustration as he tried to get the best angle for maximum pleasure —he knew what he liked and figured Xavier would like it too. Reaching between them, Xavier flicked open the buttons of his jeans, giving Vincent more room to work.

Shifting, Xavier rested his head on Vincent's shoulder, an intimate act that touched a tender part of Vincent—a piece of himself he hid from most people—and let him carry on.

Xavier trusted Vincent enough to let him do this.

Vincent watched Xavier's expression while pumping his cock. First sliding his fingers all the way to the base of him to tease his balls, then retreating to run his thumb around the tip of him where droplets of precome had emerged. Xavier shuddered against him, his hips moving in rhythm with Vincent's hand.

"Vincent," Xavier murmured, his thrusts erratic as he chased his orgasm.

Wrapping his fingers around his cock again, Vincent tightened his grip and moved his hand up and down.

Xavier panted, his eyes squeezed shut and his hips lurching in a desperate race to the finish line.

"Oh, fuck," Xavier moaned as his cock pulsed hard in Vincent's grip, warm come spilled out over Vincent's hand. Vincent didn't stop his efforts. Sliding his hand down again, he rolled Xavier's balls, and earned himself another groan and pulse of come.

"Damn," Xavier whispered, "a man could get used to that."

Lifting his head, Xavier straightened and licked into Vincent's mouth again, a deep, hot, claiming kiss that had his knees shaking—as if he wasn't already close to collapsing onto the hardwood.

Xavier broke the kiss. For a moment they stared into each other's eyes. Vincent wondered what Xavier was seeing, and whatever it was, he hoped Xavier liked it.

"Let's get cleaned up. Then have a quick beer with me so you have something to tell Romy if she ambushes you."

He pulled up his sweats and tucked himself back in. "You have beer? You hate beer."

Xavier was heading to the powder room or whatever it was called. "I bought some to have for when you came over," he said before disappearing inside the little room.

Vincent blinked, touched that Xavier had thought about him, had actually bought beer for him. It was such a small thing really, but Vincent suspected it was a big gesture for Xavier. Since returning to Cooper Springs, he'd presented himself as an all-knowing, experienced, world-weary person, a wheeler and dealer. And maybe Xavier was all those things. But he also wasn't as jaded or hard-hearted as he presented.

Taking the wet wipe Xavier held out, Vincent cleaned off his hands and followed him into the kitchen.

"You're awfully quiet. Do you want a beer?" Xavier asked.

Vincent smiled at him, embarrassed that he'd gotten lost in thought. "Yes, sorry. Was getting my brain back online."

"Bah, brains, more trouble than they're worth."

Opening the fridge, Xavier reached in and brought out a bottle of wine and a beer. He handed the beer to Vincent, saying, "I hope it's one you like. There were a lot to choose from."

It could've been flavored water and Vincent wouldn't have cared. But, in fact, the beer was one of his favorites: Primeval Stout, from a brewery up in Port Orchard.

"Thanks. This is one of my favorites."

After pouring himself a hefty serving of white wine, Xavier raised his glass to Vincent. "A toast to study hall, extra credit, and hot shop teachers."

Rolling his eyes, Vincent clinked the beer bottle against Xavier's glass. "How about one to irritating and irresistible sexy real estate agents who have a fluid definition of rules?"

"Ooh, irresistible and sexy? I'll take that. Wanna sit down? I don't know about you but I'm still feeling a bit wobbly."

Heading back into the living room, Xavier flopped down onto the couch. He patted the spot next to him. "Sit. I won't bite—not tonight anyway." Those eyebrows waggled and Vincent couldn't say no. Not that he wanted to.

Lebowski, who'd ignored their shenanigans and had opted to

nap on his dog bed, grunted and rolled onto his back, his feet sticking up into the air.

"I see he's having real issues settling in," Vincent commented dryly as he made himself comfortable next to Xavier.

"Right?" Xavier sipped his wine. "The name is perfect for him. Although I suspect if someone did break in, he wouldn't scare them off, he'd just try to get them to give him treats and shed all over them."

"They'd never get it out of their clothing. The dog hair would be evidence." Something that had been rattling around in his brain for a while resurfaced. "So, why did you move back to Cooper Springs anyway? Of all the places in the world, why back here?"

SEVENTEEN

XAVIER

Biting his lip, Xavier scooted around so he could see Vincent's handsome face better. Was it too soon to drape his legs across Vincent's lap? Damn, he wanted to cuddle. Which was entirely out of the ordinary.

"You don't have to tell me. I'm just curious is all."

Xavier snorted, Vincent deserved an honest answer. Out of habit, he swirled his wine glass, sniffing before he took another sip and let the oaky flavor slip down his throat.

"When things blew up with Arsen, I knew I needed to make a change."

Vincent's nose wrinkled at the mention of his ex.

"Agreed. But I didn't want to make a big deal of breaking up. He'd kind of branded us as a 'power couple.' Instead of giving him a laundry list of the many reasons we were over, I made my leaving about Cooper Springs. Told him it was time for me to make a difference, do something with my life instead of wining and dining clients who had the money to buy million-plus dollar properties and not bat an eye. Arsen had—and still has—a lot of clout in the industry where we lived, and the last thing I wanted was him spreading a bunch of rumors and hurting my future business."

"He's such an asshole," Vincent grumbled, taking another swallow of his beer.

"He really is," Xavier agreed. "My reasons aren't that far from reality. Mom isn't getting any younger and she refuses to move away. Max isn't moving back here, so it was up to me. It wasn't an easy decision by any means. My memories of Cooper Springs weren't that great." He touched his scarred eyebrow. "The only time I was brave enough to date I got this." He didn't know if Vincent had heard about that incident. Xavier had gone to the ER in Aberdeen, so possibly not. And he'd left for college just a few weeks later.

Scowling, Vincent set his beer down and dragged Xavier's legs so they hung over his lap. Retrieving his beer with one hand, he left his other large palm resting on Xavier's thigh—warm and reassuring. It was exactly what Xavier'd secretly wanted, but it also scared the crap out of him. Ignoring the mix of anxiety and pleasure in his stomach, he continued.

"Long story short, when I saw this house, I knew it was perfect—even if it's a bit big for a bachelor. Three bedrooms. What am I going to do with all this space anyway? But I decided to put my money where my big fat mouth is. Which means that since the move I've been searching for ways Cooper Springs can be revitalized—but still maintain its quirky character."

Vincent squeezed his thigh. "News flash, I like your big fat mouth."

His hot shop teacher neighbor was well on the way to ruining Xavier forever. His heart, an organ that normally minded its own damn business, skipped a beat at the compliment.

"That's why I'm so excited about the sale of the resort. I think Martin Purdy is perfect for Cooper Springs. If I had been skeptical of his intentions, I wouldn't have made such a big deal about the appraisal. And that's also why I invited my friend Tim down for a visit. He's a good guy, between projects, and looking for a change."

"That's impressive. I'll admit, I'm kind of jealous. After living here all my life, I've basically done nothing."

Xavier drew his eyebrows together. "You've raised an awesome kid. And even though I'm not a parent, I *know* you're a great teacher and great teachers impact kids forever. Do you remember Mr. Pinkerton?"

Vincent met his gaze and they both laughed.

"Mr. Pinkerton," Vincent said. "I hadn't thought about him in years. High and tight Marine haircut, always wore a suit and tie. Sophomore social studies. He was scary as heck but also one of the kindest teachers I ever had. Observant, always a thoughtful word even for the 'troubled' kids in class."

"And," Xavier continued, "now that I've been here a while, I'm coming to understand how much Cooper Springs has changed for the better. The people who stayed—you, Forrest and Lani, Magnus, Levi, Liam, my mom." He waved a hand to encompass those he'd forgotten. "You've made it a better place. A welcoming place. My experience has restored my faith in humanity, but don't tell anyone else, they'll think I'm getting soft."

"Hah, no one who knows you thinks that. And besides, we still have our share of the bad stuff. Rufus and his Sasquatch sightings are harmless. Finding human remains is not going to bring people to town though."

"Actually," Xavier said, grimacing, "it probably will. Just not the ones we want. If Chief Dear can't solve this—and nothing against his experience, but the odds are low—some amateur crime podcaster will decide they need to get involved." He pulled his feet off Vincent's lap and sat up. "Did you hear they finally identified the foot that washed up outside of Port Angeles a few years ago? Investigators used crowdfunding to get it tested for DNA, or whatever those forensics types do."

What Xavier didn't tell Vincent was that he'd donated a chunk of change to the cause. The anonymous foot, still in a sneaker, washing up on shore had bothered him for years, so when they'd asked for money, he'd happily given it.

"Wow, I hadn't heard. Someone's family finally has closure, very good. Hey." Vincent leaned close, squeezing his thigh again. Xavier could get used that kind of touch. To Vincent's touch. "I really should get home."

"Fine, I get it," he groused. "Thanks for letting me ambush you."

Vincent stood up and so did Xavier.

"I was happy to be ambushed." Raising his beer to his lips, he quickly swallowed the last drops. Watching his throat move, Xavier forced himself not to allow sexy thoughts.

"See you at the game tomorrow," Vincent said, his hand on the doorknob.

"See you at the game," Xavier echoed.

The door swung shut behind Vincent. Xavier stepped to the window to watch Vincent jog across the street. The lights were on in Liam's yard again, but he didn't seem to be outside. Lebowski padded over, nudging Xavier's hand with his cold doggy nose.

"Time for bed?" Xavier asked. He wasn't that tired but surely there was something he could watch for an hour or two.

By the time Xavier made it up the stairs, Lebowski was already curled up in the spot he claimed on the bed. Xavier didn't bother telling him to get down; he liked having Lebowski keep him company.

Friday it poured down all day, an absolute torrent. Upstairs in his bedroom Xavier was glumly staring at his selection of footwear. It was too late for him to drive into Aberdeen to buy a more practical pair of shoes, shoes meant for this kind of weather. He couldn't be late for kickoff; he'd never hear the end of it from Vincent.

The golden Alessandro Galet Scritto leather oxfords Arsen had gifted him for his fortieth birthday caught his eye. He paused. Could he? Should he? No, he probably shouldn't. They were gorgeous but even Xavier, shoe whore that he was, hadn't been able to wrap his brain around a pair of shoes costing over two grand. He loved well-made suits and crisp linen shirts, but he'd never forgotten his roots. At heart he was a poor country boy who'd faked his way until he'd made it.

He'd never been able to wear the damn shoes and certainly never would in Cooper Springs, not for any practical reason. Wearing them to the football game was the ultimate fuck-you to Arsen though. Arsen would never know but Xavier would, and the memory would make him happy.

"Sorry, buddy." Xavier scratched the top of Lebowski's head. "You're on guard duty tonight."

Lebowski shot him a look as he clomped over and aggressively hopped up on the bed and stared at him.

"Tomorrow we'll walk down to the shop and say hi to Mom."

As if Lebowski knew who "Mom" was, he wiggled the end of his tail. It was probably the magic word, "walk," but who knew? Maybe he did understand that Mom was someone important to Xavier. The weather was supposed to clear up too, at least for part of the day. Maybe he'd be able to convince Vincent to go with them.

Xavier thought he'd given himself plenty of time for the drive to the stadium where all the region's high schools played. It was normally about forty minutes, but the road conditions were nasty. When he finally pulled into the parking lot, there were only minutes to spare before kickoff. Grabbing his phone and checking again that he was as protected from the elements as he could be,

Xavier climbed out of his car and jogged to the stadium entrance. Vincent had said he'd be sitting with teaching staff near the fifty-yard line. Xavier spotted him almost immediately, his broad shoulders filling out the yellow slicker Xavier admired. He'd claimed a seat at the end of a row and there was an empty spot next to him. It made Xavier's heart do a thing; that was *his* spot.

"Hey," he said, sitting down next to Vincent. "Sorry I cut it so close."

"You made it. I thought maybe with the weather…"

Xavier shoulder-bumped him. "I promised I'd be here. Now," he said, looking out at the field, "what are the rules again?"

Vincent opened his mouth, snapping it shut as he realized Xavier was teasing him.

"The rules are we are only positive. Even when these massive farm boys grind our skinny coastal players into the turf and win by fifty points."

"Fifty points?"

The small crowd roared as the Sasquatch kicked off and the team did the running after the ball thing where they eventually ended up in a pile scrabbling for the ball. Xavier winced when one of their players smacked into a blue brick wall and landed flat on his back. The blue guy who'd caught the kickoff made it to mid-field before he was stopped. It took four Sasquatch players to take him down. Vincent was right, it didn't look good.

"Ouch. What are those guys eating for breakfast that our guys aren't?"

"Who knows? Maybe they get more sunlight."

Other than Vincent it was impossible to tell who else from Cooper Springs was in attendance. Everyone was huddled into anonymous rain wear, doing their best to stay dry. He was kind of surprised how many people had showed up on a rainy night.

By halftime, the Sasquatch were only down by twenty-one points, 21-42. The muddy field seemed to be working in their favor as they'd returned two kickoffs for touchdowns when opposing players slipped and missed the ball. Xavier was freezing. He'd scooted as close as he dared to Vincent. The warmest place on his body was where their thighs touched.

"Do you want a soda and some overpriced popcorn? Or we could spring for Cup 'O Noodles," Vincent asked. "My butt is getting cold sitting here."

"Sounds good to me. My whole self is cold." Xavier stood up to stretch, stiff from sitting still for so long. Vincent let out a loud scoffing sound.

"What are those shoes you're wearing?" he asked. "You do realize we're in Elma, not New York City?"

"These old things?" Xavier paused and lifted one foot, rotating it to better show off the designer shoe. "Arsen gave them to me. I've never had an occasion to wear them before." Stepping out of the row, he started to climb back up the steep stairs to the entrance level.

"They're gonna get trashed," Vincent said from behind him.

Xavier didn't reply. Vincent would get there, he was a smart man. Stepping onto the throughway where throngs of game attendees were swarming to the relative warmth and dryness of the concessions area, he waited for Vincent. He'd thought he might feel out of place or nervous, but he didn't. The few people he recognized from around town didn't bat an eye at his presence at the game. And a couple of them even smiled and waved.

"Ahh," Vincent drawled when he caught back up with him. "You don't care if the fancy shoes are ruined?"

"Bingo."

"If Arsen knew he'd probably shit bricks?"

"Platinum bricks."

Xavier stood off to one side while Vincent ordered for them. That the students all liked him was obvious. One of the teens was talking a mile a minute—although Xavier couldn't make out what she was saying—and her hands were all over the place. When she handed him their drinks, she almost tipped them over, but Vincent steadied them before there was a disaster. Waving vigorously, she smiled at him again before helping the next person in line.

"Sort-of fresh popcorn and hot chocolate," Vincent said as he handed him a paper cup and bag of popcorn.

Xavier gratefully wrapped his cold fingers around the warm cup, releasing a small sigh of pleasure.

"Twenty bucks for two popcorns and two hot chocolates," Vincent groused. "It's highway robbery but the money goes to a good cause."

"You, Vincent Barone, are a popular teacher," Xavier said. "I feel like I should be shocked, but I'm really not."

They were strolling back out to where they could see the field but were still underneath the overhang, protected from the relentless elements.

"I don't know about that," Vincent protested. "I just do my job."

"I know it." Setting his hot chocolate on the railing, Xavier opened the bag of popcorn, grabbed a handful of the stuff, and tossed it into his mouth.

Leaning his elbows against the railing, Vincent frowned. "I'm not the teacher kids crowd around, and believe me, I don't want to be. But I guess I have earned a certain level of trust. It's not like shop is rocket science, but I do hold them to deadlines. The worst for me is when they take the machine test and I have to trust no fingers will be lost."

"I can see that. Why did you go into teaching anyway?"

As the words left his mouth, the announcer came on the speakers and Vincent didn't respond.

"Before everyone sits back down to enjoy the rest of the game, we'd like to have a moment of silence for the as yet unidentified remains found on Crook's Trail last week. Know that whoever you are, local authorities are doing their best to identify you and bring you home where you belong."

Astoundingly, the entire stadium fell silent for an entire minute.

"Thank you," the announcer said.

"Wow," said Xavier. "I didn't expect that."

"I didn't either," agreed Vincent.

Another minute later, the teams took to the field again, the tiny and less-tiny figures running out to take their places.

"Let's head back to our seats," Vincent said, gesturing to the stairway.

The game ended with the Sasquatch only losing by thirty points. They'd even intercepted a pass and run it back for a touchdown. For being the losing team, they seemed in high spirits as they headed back to the locker room.

Xavier was genuinely surprised by how much he'd enjoyed watching the game. The best part had been pretending he didn't know what was happening and having Vincent calmly explain the play or call—until he figured out what Xavier was doing and started rolling his eyes instead of answering him. Seriously though, who'd come up with football terms? *Man on man coverage* was definitely his favorite.

They were walking out of the stadium when they heard Romy yelling for them to wait up.

"Hi, Xavier. Hey, Dad." Romy was bundled up in a brown and orange Sasquatch hoodie with a wool beanie pulled down over her ears. Her nose was pink from the cold, but she looked like she'd had fun too. Her friends, girls Xavier recognized from Pizza Mart, crowded behind her.

"Hey, kiddo. What's up?" Vincent asked.

Romy glanced at Xavier and then back at her dad. "Can we get a ride home with you? We don't want to ride back with Isaac, he's talking about going to Aberdeen first."

He and Vincent had planned on heading directly to the

Donkey for their "date" once the game was over, but plans were easily adjusted. Vincent glanced at Xavier, who winked back at him. Making sure Romy and her friends were safe came first, that was a no-brainer.

"I'll meet you there?" he offered.

"Taking two cars seems silly. How about I pick you up at home after I drop these troublemakers at Violet's house? That is where you're headed?" Vincent asked Romy.

Romy nodded. "Thanks, Dad. Sorry if this is an inconvenience."

"It's fine," Xavier assured her. "Your dad and I are grabbing a drink and late dinner at the Donkey, nothing that can't wait a few minutes." If Vincent and Xavier were going to date, Xavier needed to make sure Romy knew she came first. And make sure that Vincent understood that too. If they were dating. Was a high school football game and drinks an actual date? Xavier didn't know anything anymore.

Romy grinned at him and shot him a wink. Good lord, was this what Vincent had to deal with?

"See you in a few," he said to Vincent.

EIGHTEEN

VINCENT

Xavier had changed out of his ridiculous shoes into something that looked more practical. Vincent watched him lock up and walk to the car.

"Thanks for being so understanding," Vincent said as Xavier slid into the passenger seat. "I see you changed your shoes."

"Yes, and the damn things still look just fine. I'm going to have to try harder, maybe a hike on the beach with Lebowski or something."

"Thanks for being understanding," he repeated, "about Romy and her friends."

"Why wouldn't I be understanding? You don't have to apologize for being a good parent."

"I don't know. It's just awkward, I guess. Me overthinking."

The Donkey was about as busy as Vincent expected it to be on a wet, post-game Friday night, about half-full. Magnus wasn't behind the bar, but he was sitting with his dad at the end of the bar while the Friday night bartender, Garth, poured drinks, took dinner orders, and chatted with customers.

"Where do you want to sit?" Vincent asked.

Xavier glanced around before gesturing toward an empty two-top. "Let's sit there so no one can join us. No offense to our friends, but this is supposed to be a date and open seats invite the likes of Magnus."

"True." Vincent couldn't help smiling. Xavier was right about empty seats being an invitation.

"Are you really ready for this?" Xavier asked him quietly. "It's my past making me anxious, but once you're really out—not just Magnus shooting us knowing looks—there's no putting the cat back into the bag."

Vincent started toward the table, knowing Xavier would follow him.

When they arrived, he held his hand out to Xavier. "Your coat, please?"

A bemused expression on his face, Xavier unzipped his parka and handed it to Vincent. Had no one ever treated Xavier like he was something special? Not just a date spending money to make themself look good, but *special* to them? Taking the coat, Vincent hung it up on a nearby hook. Xavier moved to sit down. Scowling at him, Vincent stepped over and pulled out his chair for him.

"Yes," Vincent said, taking the seat opposite, "I am ready."

Garth stopped by their table and took their drink orders. Vincent glanced around to see that no one was paying them any attention. Magnus seemed to be deep in a conversation with his dad, and the rest of the crowd was enjoying their food and drink. Orville Peck was playing overhead, crooning about how the town not being big enough for the two of them. Vincent didn't listen to music often but *Let Me Drown* was a perennial on his driving playlist.

But, for Xavier and Vincent at least, the lyric's sentiment wasn't true anymore, was it? The heart of Cooper Springs was big enough and growing bigger every day. Maybe it didn't look like it from the outside. There was a lot of work to do. But Vincent knew in *his* heart it could be done.

"Are you okay?" Vincent asked.

"Yeah, I'm great. Really great."

Vincent leaned back in his chair. "Good, you had me worried for a second."

"Sorry, I was just thinking."

"Good things, I hope?"

"The best."

"You asked why I went into teaching."

"I did."

Without interrupting, Garth set their drinks in front of them. Lifting his glass, Xavier swirled the golden liquid. Two weeks ago, Vincent would have thought he was pretentious and showing off but no longer. This was just pure Xavier Stone.

"You know that old saying," Vincent continued, turning his pint glass so he could see the logo, "about how those who can do and those who can't teach? To be honest, that pisses me off. But when I was in college, both my parents were elderly, and I knew they wouldn't be around for much longer. The other quote about teaching is 'three words, June, July and August' and that one is valid. I figured if I could get a teaching job at the high school—and believe me, they are always looking for male teachers—it would be that much easier to take care of them. I wasn't going to leave town, and summer vacation gave us quality time to spend together."

"I'm impressed. Tell me about them. I don't think I ever met your parents, but they raised a good person."

When he was a kid, Vincent had sometimes been embarrassed by his parents. Their English was rusty at best, and heavily accented. They dressed funny. And they were older than his friends' parents by a lot. There weren't many new parents in their midforties in the 1980s, and they had old country habits that, until he'd started school, Vincent hadn't known were not the norm. It had been a shock to learn not everyone buried statues in their yard for good luck or made everything from scratch, including breakfast cereal.

"They emigrated here in the seventies. Don't ask me how they managed it because I don't know, and they never told me. I do know they settled in Cooper Springs when they got here, and Dad started up with the fleet."

The fleet was what townies called the men who risked their lives fishing in the capricious waters of the Pacific. The small fleets were a thing of the past these days, especially after so many had perished when a freak storm blew in, surprising the fishermen.

"Anyway, Dad spent his days fishing, and Mom tended a huge garden that fed us, and more."

"Didn't they have a fruit stand too?"

"We did, up until the end of high school. Then it became too much, and my mom's health was failing fast."

"They sound like good people."

"They were very good people." Vincent smiled thinking about them. Still very glad they'd never known about Carly. "But we're not here to talk about me, or my parents. Not *all* about me anyway."

He started when the front entrance flew open. A gust of wind must've caught the door because the guy coming in fought to pull it shut behind him.

"Do you know him?" Xavier asked.

"Dante Brown. He's new to town, his niece is in one of my classes."

"Huh."

"What huh?"

"Nothing huh, just huh."

Brown strode to the bar and leaned on it as he waited for

Garth to take his order. Vincent wondered what he did for a living. The man may have appeared to be focused on the bartender, but Vincent sensed he was hyperaware of his surroundings.

"Is he a cop?" Xavier wondered.

Vincent shrugged. "I didn't ask him. What parents and guardians do for a living isn't any of my business unless it's illegal."

The door opened again, and this time it was Liam Wright who came inside, followed by Nicholas Waugh. Liam shot Vincent a fast wink but didn't approach their table.

Nicholas looked better than he had last time Vincent had seen him, out at the resort, but not by much. Nick was still skinny and the bags under his eyes had luggage tags on them. His clothes were rumpled, even for Cooper Springs. There was no public place in Cooper Springs to do laundry, the Laundr-O-Mat having been one of the businesses that disappeared along with the timber mill.

"What this town really needs is an accessible laundry," Xavier said, his gaze following Vincent's.

Xavier had a point. Nick Waugh wasn't the only one without access to a washer and dryer.

"We could use one. Any brilliant thoughts, idea guy?"

Xavier laughed. "Sorry, my brain. I saw some on a trip in Iceland a few years ago. Gas stations with oversized industrial washers and dryers that were outside for anyone to use. They weren't free, of course. But, I dunno, I can't be the only one who enjoys wearing clean clothes and sleeping on clean sheets. It doesn't seem like it would be impossible, does it?"

Vincent's gaze flicked to Nick and back to Xavier. "Probably not?" It wouldn't hurt to ask around, although Vincent thought there was as about as much chance of funding an outdoor public laundry as getting town leaders to refresh The Strip with hanging flower baskets in the spring and summer, or even repainting the crosswalks.

"But seeing our resident chainsaw artist reminds me I need to make time to talk to the mayor and her cronies about my ideas I have for bringing tourists to town. *Plans,* really, because these are good ideas and I know people will come."

There was a gleam in Xavier's eye that Vincent was learning not to ignore. "What idea?"

Please don't say Extreme Chainsaw Shakespeare.

"I told you before," he said. "An Extreme Chainsaw Shake-speare competition in the spring—and Shakespeare on the Beach in August. Magnus can revisit his role as Prospero."

Groaning, Vincent leaned back in his chair, his imagination taking him on an unpleasant trip to the closest emergency room where damaged eyeballs were being examined and limbs were being reattached. He shot Xavier his best WTF stare as he took a long deep swallow of his beer. The look didn't appear to phase Xavier at all.

Of course it didn't.

Xavier leaned across the table, his eyes wide and excitement palatable. "What if you were the head of the safety committee? Obviously, contestants will have to sign a safety waiver but there's other stuff. Like, I don't know... how far away will the people who come to watch have to stand? Will the artists actually carve during the contest? Will they bring finished art to sell? Stuff like that."

He sat up again, waving a hand as he kept going. "Maybe there could be a main stage where contestants carve and visitors watch them, but they can also have separate booths. And atten-dees could vote on their favorites. The winner gets some prize money, and the rest of the proceeds would be donated to a specific Cooper Springs-oriented charity? I haven't thought much past that yet."

"You've thought plenty," Vincent grumbled. "Why couldn't

you have come up with something safe, like face painting or juggling?"

Instead of replying, Xavier brought out his cell phone and began pressing the screen.

"What are you doing?"

"Reminding myself to make an appointment with the mayor next week, or as soon as she has time. But first I'm going to research permitting, I need to be as prepared as possible." He glanced up. "Can I tell Roslyn you're on board?"

Throwing his head back, Vincent stared up at the dark wooden beams that made up the ceiling of The Steam Donkey. The lumber they'd used for the ceiling and the rest of the building had been harvested directly from the surrounding forest. Maybe the trees had even stood on this site before August Cooper had decided to build a timber mill, and therefore a town, in a remote area on the Washington coastline.

Lowering his head, Vincent stared across the table. Xavier stared back at him. His golden-brown eyes were full of hope and excitement for the future of Cooper Springs, but there was uncertainty there too. As if he wanted Vincent's approval. As if it meant something to him.

Vincent was, in a word, fucked.

He realized at that moment, barring breaking the law—and who knew, maybe that too— he would do anything for Xavier Stone. The list of people he felt that way about had doubled to two in the past few weeks. Damn.

"I'll think about it."

"Yes!" Smiling ever harder, Xavier jabbed the air with a fist before raising his glass and chinking it against Vincent's. "To the promising future of Cooper Springs!"

That was a toast Vincent was happy to make. "To the future of Cooper Springs," he echoed.

He tossed back the rest of his beer and set the glass down on the table. Xavier was watching him, his gaze darkened.

"What?" Vincent asked.

"You want to head back to my place?"

Vincent stood up, grabbed his coat, and handed Xavier his.

"Yes."

Tossing him a fabulous grin, Xavier pulled on his coat and turned toward the door.

NINETEEN
XAVIER

Xavier

Shivering, Xavier tucked his chin down into his parka in a vain attempt to keep warm. He'd neglected to wrap a scarf around his neck, and he deeply regretted it. It was fucking cold. The wind had blown last night's cloud cover east, exposing a gorgeous robin's-egg blue sky but bringing temperatures down to barely above freezing. Vincent trudged along beside him, his broad shoulders hunched, and both his hands shoved deep into his coat pockets. At least the hand Xavier had shoved into his pocket was warm.

In front of them, at the end of his leash, Lebowski darted back and forth, his tail wagging and nose skimming the ground, snuffling and sniffing. What he was tracking, Xavier had no idea. During high tides, this section of the route to the beach was often covered in brackish water. Hence the bridge he and Vincent had gotten into an argument over.

Technically, the path wasn't public access, but Mr. Davies had never minded the townspeople using it. Probably Lebowski was smelling fishy things that had been left behind by the retreating ocean.

Vincent had spent the night. Xavier let a satisfied smile play across his lips. Their first "real" date *and* a sleepover. Xavier suspected he might be able to get used to Vincent in his bed— and the rest of his life. And, for once, it didn't scare the crap out of him.

When he'd woken this morning, he'd waited for a feeling of dread to creep over him followed by second-guessing. But, after laying there for a while and listening to Vincent's deep, sleepy breathing, he'd realized he felt fine. Happy, even. He'd certainly never felt that way with Arsen, neither of them having been willing to let their guard down long enough for real feelings to become involved.

A couple hundred yards in front of them, waves crashed violently against the wide expanse of sandy beach. The rhythmic pounding echoed off the bluffs on either side. To his right, Xavier could just see the corner of one of the resort cabins, tucked under swaying sixty-foot fir trees. Seabirds, mostly gulls, but also sandpipers and crows, hunted for snacks above the tide line.

Unexpectedly, Lebowski bolted, and his leash ripped from Xavier's grip.

"Lebowski! Get back here!" Xavier's command was carried away by the wind. Lebowski, who over the past few days had proven he could hear a bag of treats being opened through closed doors, kept running.

"Lebowski!" Vincent yelled, starting to run too.

They raced after the dog. Xavier began to worry they would be chasing him up the beach to god knew where when Lebowski halted at the accursed bridge and started to bark at something.

"What the actual fuck," Xavier huffed as they closed in on the escapee. He grabbed the end of the leash before checking to see what Lebowski was going on about.

"Mother trucker. Xavier."

Vincent's grim tone had him immediately on edge.

"What?"

Xavier had a vivid imagination, but even he didn't expect Vincent's next words.

"It's not a what, it's a who. Did you bring your phone? We need to call the police."

Wrapping the loose end of the leash around his wrist and dragging Lebowski to his side, Xavier crossed to where Vincent was standing, his attention focused downward. Xavier followed his gaze to the shallow and, tragically, not entirely empty estuary.

A body haphazardly lay below them, half-exposed to the elements, half-snagged underneath the footbridge. Jean-clad legs were visible, a sneaker on one foot, the other bare. The rest of whoever it was, was hidden from view.

"Keep a hold of the dog," Vincent ordered, starting down the slope.

"What are you doing?"

"Checking for a pulse."

Something told Xavier the person was dead and had been for a while. It was too cold, and last night it had been even colder. Hypothermia worked quickly in the wind and frigid air. He and Max had both experienced it when they were young and stupid.

Vincent reached the bottom, moving in a crouch to peer under the bridge. A second later he looked back up at Xavier, his expression grim and his head moving back and forth.

"Who is it?" Xavier asked. "Anyone we know?"

"Lizzy Harlow."

Chief Dear and Deputy Cooper stared morosely down at Lizzy Harlow's body. They hadn't moved her yet, but Chief Dear had climbed down to confirm what they already knew. She was dead.

Xavier, Vincent, and Lebowski waited off to one side, as out of the way as they could, but they could hear the conversation.

Lebowski had resumed his easygoing persona, hanging out next to Xavier's side while the chief and deputy decided how best to approach the scene.

"Honestly, I'm not sure why I thought a small town would be less stress," Dear muttered.

"You didn't think to ask me," Lani replied. "There's a reason I didn't apply for the job."

Scowling, Andre shot his deputy a glare before scowling even harder at the body.

"Did you know her?" he asked.

Lani nodded. "Hard not to know Lizzy."

While they'd waited for the police, Vincent had told Xavier that she'd run in the same disreputable circles as Vincent's ex-wife. But who she was friends with didn't mean she deserved her fate, or that she wouldn't be missed by someone.

"Lizzy Harlow. Why do I know that name?" asked Andre, frowning again.

Lani stomped her boots in an attempt to keep warm. "You drove Jayden Harlow home the other day."

"Right, that's where I've heard it before. But his mother wasn't home. Dammit all to hell. Standing here isn't going to get us closer to figuring out who did this." He turned to Xavier and Vincent. "It's going to be a hot minute. We'll need to wait for the coroner and collect as much evidence as we can before releasing the scene. How do you feel about meeting us at the station later for your statements?"

"Sure, Chief," agreed Xavier.

"Who's checking on the kids?" Vincent asked. "Jayden and Abby? Their dad is in the Navy and not home much."

"This day just keeps getting better and better," Andre grunted. His gaze moved from Lizzy Harlow's body to the cloudless sky and then to his deputy. "Cooper, we'll have to call in Trent and have him make the trip."

Lani wrinkled her nose, and Andre shrugged. Xavier suppressed a snort.

"Alternatively," Vincent began, hesitant, "I could ride along with Trent. I'd rather drink the battery acid the Stop-N-Go calls coffee, but it's better than Lionel Trent showing up alone. No offense to Lionel," he said to the Chief, "but he's not a people person."

Deputy Lionel Trent was around sixty, and every cliché about small-town cops applied to him—possibly existed because of him. He was sexist, obliquely racist, and homophobic. He was pissed the city hadn't tapped him for the job when the previous chief moved on. Xavier figured Andre was just waiting for him to retire.

There was no love lost between Trent and Xavier. He'd been the single responding cop when Xavier had been jumped by his date all those years ago and had brushed the whole thing off as a misunderstanding. A lesson Xavier had never forgotten.

"That's why he's got permanent night shift," Lani muttered. "Worse, even though he's been a cop for years, he's a clumsy oaf at crime scenes."

"Jayden is a ninth grader," Vincent added. "I don't have him in any classes, but he probably knows who I am."

"It's against my better judgment but I'm starting to realize things happen a little differently out here. Cooper, give Trent the heads-up. Have him pick up Barone and head out there. Tell him there's no need for a siren and lights, the kids are going to be traumatized enough without him barging in."

Sketching out a mock salute, Lani turned and started back toward the cruiser she'd had to park in the resort parking lot. "Somebody's gonna have to notify Corey Harlow too," she called over her shoulder.

Xavier did not envy the person who had to tell Corey Harlow his wife was dead. Did the Harlows have any relatives left in town? Where were the kids going to stay? How long would it take for Corey to get back to Cooper Springs from wherever he was?

Vincent quickly squeezed Xavier's arm. "See you as soon as I can."

Yeah, because who knew how long this would take.

Vincent jogged after Lani and Xavier sighed, trying not to feel resentful that Lizzy Harlow had turned up dead on their walk.

Chief Dear cocked his head at him. "You can go too."

"Do you want me to wait until Lani—I mean, Deputy Cooper —gets back? Truthfully, I am fucking freezing. And to be honest, not really a fan of corpses, but I'll do my civic duty and stick around if you need me to. Aren't you supposed to be taking pictures and"—he waved his warmer hand—"stuff?"

He'd been avoiding looking at Lizzy Harlow's body again. What he had seen was already permanently etched in his memory.

Andre shot him a dry look. "I appreciate the offer, but the coroner will be here soon enough. And Cooper isn't going anywhere, she's just waiting for Trent to arrive."

Dismissed, Xavier tugged on Lebowski's leash, and they began heading back toward The Strip.

Walking slowly behind Lebowski, his thoughts swirled along with the bitter wind. How had Lizzy Harlow ended up under the bridge? Had she decided to go on a beach walk in the night with no coat? And what had happened to her other shoe? Had she been drunk or high and made her last bad decision? And fuck, her kids, they must be scared.

"Stone! What the fuck is going on?"

Xavier halted. Dammit. He'd forgotten about Nick Waugh. And Martin Purdy, who needed to know a body had been found on his almost-property.

Nick stormed toward him. He'd obviously seen the police cars and they all knew he took his guard duties seriously. Fuck.

Stopped a few feet away, Nick eyed Lebowski. He had no way of knowing the dog wouldn't hurt a fly.

"Are you gonna tell me what's going on or do I have to talk to the cop?"

Glancing back over his shoulder and then at Nick again, Xavier weighed his choices. Probably Lani and Andre would talk to him anyway, but it might be better if he broke the news. Frankly, Xavier was surprised there weren't more townies crowding the scene, demanding to know what the police were doing at the resort.

"There's a body under the bridge. Lebowski found it when we were walking."

Nick frowned. "Lebowski?"

"My dog," Xavier clarified, shaking the leash.

"Who is it?" Nick demanded, nodding in Chief Dear's direction, his tone belligerent. Xavier wasn't sure he had any other.

Xavier sighed. Deciding Nick was boring, Lebowski padded over to lean against Xavier's thigh. Fucking small towns, why had he moved back here again? He glanced over his shoulder. Chief Dear was watching them, hands on his hips as the realization that the investigation was already out of his control set in. What Xavier needed was a cup of coffee, not to be interrogated by grumpy Nick Waugh.

"Just tell me. I'm not going to spread it around."

True that. Nick was not a member of the town gossip club.

"It might be Lizzy Harlow." Screw it. "It is Lizzy."

"Lizzy?" Nick narrowed his eyes. "What was she doing out there?"

"I guess that's for Chief Dear to find out."

"Was it an accident?"

"Look, Nick, I am not a cop. I don't know. I guess we'll all find out soon enough."

"Huh," Nick grunted. "I suppose not even a dead body will keep that asshole from buying the resort."

Xavier rolled his eyes. Seriously? What the fuck was Nick's problem with Martin Purdy?

"The sale officially closes in ten days. Martin Purdy is not backing out. He's already accepted an offer on his house in Seattle and booked a moving truck. He'll be here before Thanksgiving."

His attention on Chief Dear, Nick said, "I guess it was too much to hope he'd back out. I don't have that kind of luck."

"Look, Nick, get over yourself. The sale is done, there's nothing left to talk about. I'm freezing. I need a hot cup of coffee and the town needs people like Martin Purdy. People who look at Cooper Springs and see something promising—a future. He's not tearing it down, he's planning on remodeling and renting the cabins again. This is a good thing for the town, the first good thing to happen in a while."

Nick's jaw clenched and he stepped into Xavier's space. Lifting one fingerless-glove-clad hand, Nick poked Xavier in the chest hard enough he felt each jab through his thick coat.

"Something funny is going on around town and I'm going to find out what. You all laugh at me, tell me I'm paranoid. But you won't be laughing when murder interferes with your hoity-toity plans."

Without giving Xavier a chance to reply, Nick turned his back and headed back in the direction he'd come from.

"That went well, don't you think, Lebowski?"

Lebowski obviously agreed with him. He gave Xavier's hand an enthusiastic lick and tugged on his leash, ready to go home.

TWENTY
VINCENT

Vincent didn't dislike many people. It wasn't worth his energy. He very much disliked Lionel Trent. Instead of spending the morning with Xavier and Lebowski, maybe heading back to Xavier's for a warm cup of coffee and offering to make his signature homemade waffles, he was in a car with Lionel Trent, heading to Zenith to deliver the worst news he could imagine.

It took everything he had to slide into the passenger seat of Trent's cruiser, shoving aside the empty paper bags and coffee cups that littered the footwell so there was room for his feet.

"Just chuck it in the back."

Yeah, no, Vincent wasn't touching Trent's garbage.

Luckily for Vincent, Trent didn't seem to be in a mood for small talk. The twenty-five-minute drive was quiet, just the occasional crackle of the cruiser's radio breaking the silence.

The closer they got to Zenith the sicker to his stomach Vincent felt about Lizzy Harlow. He'd never liked her, but he'd never wished her dead. And now her kids' lives were about to be changed forever. There was no coming back from death. Vincent spent the majority of the drive wondering who they'd call if there was no emergency number on hand.

Jayden was around thirteen, but Vincent couldn't remember how old his younger sister was. The last thing he wanted was to call in social services. They meant well, but these kids were already going to be traumatized. It would be better for the siblings if they could stay in Cooper Springs with someone they trusted while they waited for their dad to arrive.

The Harlow address turned out to be one of the nicer homes in Zenith, a single-story wood structure probably built in the 1960s. The house needed a new coat of paint and the lawn was overgrown, but it was better than Vincent had expected. And either holiday lights had been hung early or they'd never come down from the year before.

Raising his fist, Trent hammered on the front door.

"What the hell?" Vincent demanded. "Are you trying to scare the kids?"

Trent just shrugged. A minute or so later, the door was opened a few inches and a sullen teen boy Vincent recognized as Jayden Harlow stared at them.

"What?" Jayden asked, his tone matching his expression.

Vincent stepped in front of Trent. "Hi, Jayden. I'm Vincent Barone, I teach at the high school. Officer Trent and I have some, um, bad news. Can we come in?"

"I know who you are," Jayden said to Vincent, still holding onto the door. "What kind of news?" His face crumpled, tears springing to his eyes. "Is it my dad? Is he dead?"

"No, it's not your dad. Can we come in? Is your sister here?"

"Abby's at a sleepover." Gripping the door handle, Jayden visibly regained his control as he backed up enough to let them inside.

Vincent took the living room in with a glance. The closed

curtains and dim overhead light couldn't hide the built-up grime. The carpet hadn't been vacuumed in forever and the lesser-used surfaces were covered with dust. Boxes were stacked along one wall. A flatscreen TV hung on the wall opposite the couch and some video game had been paused, the character in mid-jump.

Vincent had no intention of sitting on the couch.

"Jayden, do you have any relatives in Zenith or Cooper Springs?" Vincent asked.

What was the protocol about telling a minor their mother was dead? It wasn't as if the news was going to stay a secret for long.

"It's Mom, isn't it? She's dead." Jayden's voice was flat now, nothing like the emotion he'd shown when he'd thought they'd knocked on the door to tell him his dad was gone.

Vincent nodded, ashamed by the relief he felt not having to say the words. "I'm afraid so. She was found in Cooper Springs this morning."

Jayden plopped onto the couch. He seemed resigned rather than sad, almost as if he'd been expecting bad news. Vincent felt a stab of guilt that he hadn't followed through with checking in on the Harlow kids a few weeks ago. He'd allowed the budding relationship with Xavier to cloud his priorities.

"What's going to happen to us?" Jayden asked. "To me and Abby?"

Fear had overtaken resignation. Jayden was just starting to understand his life had changed forever.

"That's why I asked about relatives," Vincent said. "If we can't find anyone for you to stay with until your dad is notified and gets home, we'll be required to call in social services."

"No!" Jayden shot to his feet again. He scowled at Vincent and Deputy Trent, his fists clenched at his sides. "I can take care of Abby until Dad gets home. It's what I've been doing anyway."

Filing *that* comment away for later, Vincent said, "It's the rules. I'm sorry."

"Rules are for suckers."

Behind him, Trent cleared his throat. Vincent held up one hand. Cop or not, the last thing they needed was Trent adding his two cents.

"Maybe they are sometimes." Vincent wasn't going to argue with the kid. "But in your and Abby's case, they need to be followed. Do you know of any relatives here in Zenith or Cooper Springs? Also, we're going to need to know where your sister is right now."

"Abby's at Misha Roberts's house," Jayden said. "Her mom is going to bring her home later. Was, I guess. Um..." Jayden's gaze flicked between Vincent and the deputy. "Forrest Cooper told me to call him if I ever needed anything. He's, like, our third cousin. He said so."

Trent snorted and Vincent had to repress the urge to do the same. Forrest Cooper liked to claim he was the Kevin Bacon of Cooper Springs, only it was three degrees instead of six.

"Do you mind if we use your phone?"

"Mom didn't pay the bill. It hasn't worked for a few days."

Vincent didn't want to think poorly of the dead, but Lizzy Harlow was trying his resolve.

"Pack a bag, grab what you'll need for a few days—including your homework."

Without a word, Jayden disappeared down a short hallway adjacent to what must have been the kitchen. Vincent hoped he was grabbing clothes and not planning on sneaking out or something.

The drive back to Cooper Springs was as quiet as the drive to Zenith had been. The exception was Trent radioing Lani with Abby Harlow's whereabouts. He also asked Lani if she was related to the Harlows.

"Anything is possible, just ask my brother." Vincent heard Lani's eyeroll. Forrest Cooper was the town conspiracy theorist.

"Seriously though, family trees aren't my thing. The coroner is here now. I'll head over to Misha's and pick up Abby, meet me at the station. FYI, I called the base and got the ball rolling. They are notifying Corey Harlow ASAP. He should be home in twenty-four to forty-eight hours."

Trent clicked off without acknowledging Lani's information. Vincent frowned. Trent must be a real joy to work with. Sure, he'd been called in after night shift, but he could have made an effort not to be a jerk.

"Jayden, what does your dad do in the Navy?" he asked.

After a sullen silence, Jayden said, "I dunno. Fixes stuff."

Jayden was upset about Lizzy's death—he thought—but Vincent sensed something else there too. Anger. Was the anger aimed at his mom? His dad? Both parents? And what had his comment about taking care of Abby meant? Vincent suspected he already knew the answer but wished he didn't.

Lizzy's death meant Corey would be released from service, but how would he feel about suddenly becoming the single dad of two grieving kids? Would Corey be devastated by Lizzy's death?

Deputy Cooper had already gotten in touch with her brother. Forrest was waiting outside the station for them by the time Trent pulled the police car to the curb. Vincent didn't know what to think when Jayden scrambled out and raced across the sidewalk to Forrest, wrapping himself around the red-headed man as if he was drowning and Forrest was the only one who could save him.

Forrest appeared shocked too. He met Vincent's gaze over the top of Jayden's head, his gaze concerned.

Before they could say anything, Lani pulled up and parked behind Trent. When she opened the passenger door, Abby climbed out and ran for her brother. The two siblings clutched each other, Abby sobbing, her shoulders shaking, while Jayden was more resolute, as if he felt he needed to be strong for his younger sister. How lost and alone they must feel.

Vincent was just barely keeping himself together, and it was only because there were kids around and he was in public What would happen to Romy if something happened to him? He'd been doing his best to not to dwell on the possibility, but Lizzy's death brought his relative isolation to the front and center. Who did he have? Who did Romy have?

"Thank you, Vincent," Lani said, bringing him out of his dark thoughts.

"Sure, happy to help. Do you need me to stick around?"

"We'll need to take your statement. Do you want to do that now?"

Lani Cooper offered him a ride home, but Vincent refused. He walked quickly toward his house, needing the bitter cold wind to help clear his head. Lizzy's death had made one thing glaringly obvious to Vincent; while the time with Xavier had been good —*more than good,* even he would admit that—he needed to focus on his real life, not a fantasy. On *real* things.

Stepping away from the sexy, witty, and surprisingly tender Xavier Stone—and the nameless other things he couldn't fit into his life—was what Vincent needed to do. Romy was what mattered. He needed to distance himself from Xavier, he was an unpredictable factor. Who knew if Xavier would stick around if something happened to him? Vincent couldn't expect Xavier to take care of Romy, and he would never ask him to. Who knew if they would last that long? Life was uncertain and there was no need to invite more uncertainty into it.

The only solution was for Vincent to hunker down and focus. Save more money. Return to his practical roots. Maybe he'd look for a third job or pick up more appraisal work so he could beef up his bank account. Enough that if anything happened to him,

Romy would be safe, could take care of what she needed. She was almost old enough, there was a good chance she could get declared an emancipated minor if there was enough money in the bank.

His brain swirled a million miles a minute as he came up with solutions and then discarded them.

"Vincent! Wait up!"

Xavier's voice cut through Vincent like a knife. He couldn't pretend he hadn't heard him. He'd just turned down their block, he could see both their front yards, Xavier's quaint yard with the wrought iron fence kitty-corner from Vincent's charmless rental.

Stopping, he glanced over his shoulder. Xavier, with Lebowski in the lead, was hurrying toward him.

"Uh, hi," he said lamely when Xavier reached him. Lebowski stuck his head under Vincent's hand, and he aimlessly patted him.

"Hi to you too." Xavier raised his hand holding the leash. "Lebowski wanted to go out again," he explained. "I have fresh coffee on, do you want to come over for a cup?" He threw in a wink at the end.

If he was going to end this—whatever it was—he needed to do it now before they got too deep.

"Hmm, um. I don't think it's a good idea. Look, Xavier, I think..." He couldn't bring himself to say "break up"; they hadn't been together long enough. "I think we should slow things down. Take it easy. Maybe we've had stars in our eyes and aren't thinking straight. It's for the best. This way no one gets hurt."

Xavier's expression hardened, changing from pleasure to something Vincent couldn't read. His eyes, always expressive, shuttered. Lebowski moved away from Vincent to lean against Xavier's leg.

"What brought this on?" Xavier asked as he eyed Vincent. After a heartbeat or four, comprehension dawned. "This is about this morning, isn't it?"

Xavier didn't wait for Vincent's answer.

"I get it. I think I do anyway. This is you panicking. This is Vincent Barone getting stuck in his head. Kinda like the bridge." He winced. "Okay, bad example—but you know what I mean, worrying about everything. You're taking this incident and extrapolating so far out, you might as well have taken a shuttle to Mars."

"Worrying about my child, my child's future, is not Mars. It's not as if you have anyone you worry about."

Xavier's expression turned stony and his eyes glittered.

"Is that what you really think? That I don't have anyone? That I don't care about anyone?" Staring up at the clouds, Xavier threw up his free hand as he released an honest-to-god roar. The sound faded and Xavier lowered his head to glare at Vincent. "Fine, you can have your meltdown." He stepped in and poked his chest. "But we are not done."

With those words, Xavier tugged on Lebowski's leash and stomped across the street. Against his better judgement, Vincent waited and watched him go inside. The slamming of his front door felt very much like an end to something.

That was good, right?

TWENTY-ONE

XAVIER

Vincent was panicking. Knowing the truth didn't set Xavier free, it was making him grind his teeth. Dragging a deep breath into his lungs, Xavier held it for a second before releasing it.

Fine.

Things were going to be fine. *He* wasn't going to panic just because Vincent was experiencing a wobble over life, the universe —and discovering a corpse. It was practically predetermined, Xavier should have expected this reaction. He knew that, for Vincent—even if they hadn't been together that long—finding Lizzy Harlow had been a traumatic experience. And Vincent worried more than most people Xavier knew.

Xavier was not going to panic. That was the old Xavier. The revamped Xavier, the one who'd moved back to his hometown and had—however unwillingly—found himself drawn to the adult version of the kid who'd gotten him sent to the principal for running his underwear up the flagpole, was going to act reasonably, be patient. Daisy had called it. Damn, his cousin was sharp. And his brother, but he'd never admit it to Max.

This caretaker aspect of Vincent's personality was both the best and worst of him. Xavier didn't appreciate being lumped in the "it's just best if we call it off now" category, but he'd give Vincent time to calm down. It was possible that he'd come to his senses on his own, that he'd realize he'd acted impulsively. Just in case he didn't, Xavier needed a plan.

Lebowski whined, tugging on his leash.

"Sorry, dude."

Unclipping him, Xavier hung the leash on the coat rack. Lebowski trotted into the kitchen, then Xavier heard the sound of him getting a drink of water.

Not going to panic. Nope.

Slipping out of his coat, Xavier flung it haphazardly over the rack, took off his shoes, and followed Lebowski into the kitchen.

Panic or not, a glass of wine sounded like fucking heaven. He eyeballed his wine rack then glanced at the stove clock. 2:23. It was five o'clock somewhere, right? Happy hour anyway.

He'd just taken the first sip of an oaky, special edition, wine he'd found at a winery in Port Townsend when his landline rang.

Seriously? Already?

"Dammit."

Taking his wine with him, Xavier padded out to the living room, retrieved the handset, and settled onto the couch. Lebowski had trailed after him. He looked at Xavier and at the couch before lifting one paw and setting it on a cushion.

The phone rang in his hand. He patted the cushion and Lebowski jumped up settling in next to him. At least the dog wasn't panicking.

"Hello, Max."

"What's going on?" his brother demanded.

"Why is it always me?" Xavier wanted to know. "Why am I not the one calling you to ask questions and dig into your personal life?"

"Dunno. Spill."

There really was no way to ease into finding a body. Or explaining that the person you'd thought you hated but actually liked, and had most recently been fostering the tiniest hopeful sprouts of a future with, had ended things—or thought they had.

"The morning started off well but ended with Lebowski finding Lizzy Harlow's body over by the cabins."

Max was silent for a moment. Xavier thought he heard the muffled sound of traffic over the line. Where was he?

"Shit, that's terrible," Max said.

"Yeah," Xavier agreed. "Then, Vincent rode along with Deputy Trent to check on her kids—they're okay"—he doubted the Harlow kids were really okay, but they hadn't been physically harmed—"and by the time he got back from Zenith, he'd decided we couldn't be a *we*."

That's not what he'd said, but Xavier was going to allow himself an hour or so for personal drama.

"Was it an accident? How did she die?"

Glad Max started with questions about the body first and not Vincent Barone, Xavier thought back to the lack of a coat and only one shoe. The haphazard and unnatural abandonment of her body. It had only been five hours or so since they'd found her, and as far as he was aware investigators hadn't released any official information about what had happened. He suspected that cause of death would not be listed as *natural causes*.

"I don't know. Vincent is the one who climbed down to check for a pulse, I didn't get that close."

"Damn. I'd be freaked out too."

"Yeah." Xavier took another sip of his wine. "I'm reeling. How often do you find a body when you're taking the dog for a walk? Is this the dark secret of dog ownership I wasn't warned about?"

Max didn't reply right away. Xavier sipped more of his wine, enjoying Lebowski snuggling into his side. This was the part that was cool about being a twin, they didn't always have to talk. Even so, he was ready for the shoe to be on the other foot when it came to relationships.

"We'll fast forward past the part where I was right about you and Vincent."

Xavier rolled his eyes to the ceiling. Max could be so smug. "Whatever."

"So, you and Vincent figured things out and now Vincent wants to un-figure them?"

"He's panicking." Xavier may not have been intimate with Vincent for long, but he had a lifetime of experience reading people. "Finding a body. Telling the Harlow kids their mom was dead. It was a lot and I think he couldn't help but start thinking about his own kid and his own life, and he decided it was best to shut the gates. Protect himself and Romy."

"How would doing that protect him or Romy?"

"I didn't say it was logical." Pausing, Xavier took another sip of his wine. "Maybe he thinks it's easier to stick with what he knows. Which is he and Romy against the world, one foot in the front of the other—that sort of thing."

"That sounds lonely."

"Again, I didn't say it was logical, but it is what he's used to."

"What're you going to do about it?" Max asked.

A horn blared and was followed by another, sharper blast. Where was his brother?

"Let myself wallow for the rest of the day. Then I'll figure out how to talk to him."

The traffic sounds abruptly quieted, as if Max had been outside before and was now inside.

"Are you having dinner at Mom's tonight?"

"Are you showing up?" Xavier teased. "Not sure I can stomach your face."

No matter how old he was, it always amused him to infer his identical twin was ugly.

"Har har har. I had planned on heading over. But at the last minute I decided to hit the road today, instead of tomorrow. I'm talking to you from a motel just outside of Boise."

Xavier scowled. And Max had called *him* because he'd been sending tweaky vibes?

"Did you call Mom yet?" Xavier asked him, knowing his brother had not. Mom would have already called him with the news.

"I haven't yet, but I will. I wanted to talk to you first."

"You mean you wanted to know if I would be there when you called."

"Maybe," Max conceded. "With luck I'll make Jackson tomorrow. Collier Creek isn't far from there."

Xavier had never bothered to look up the small town their dad had come from. He was never going to visit, never planned to meet the relatives they supposedly had there. It sounded like drama, and Xavier wasn't interested.

"Brother, I do not understand this pilgrimage you've taken on."

"I know. I just feel like I need to go, I can't explain it."

Of the two of them, Max was the predictable one. Xavier had been the one who their mom had sworn several hundred times was going to drive her to drink. After a lifetime of being the good twin, it was Max's turn for the hot seat. Xavier was more than ready to pass along the mantle.

"I told her I'd be there around five."

His mom opened her door and looked past Xavier. Not seeing Vincent, she asked, "Where's Vincent? And Romy?"

"What am I? Chopped liver?"

"Come in, and you too, Lebowski," she cooed at his dog. "Mop and Berkeley missed you!"

Inside he stripped off his coat and hung it over the back of her couch.

"You heard the news?" he asked, knowing he didn't need to mention names. "I'm surprised you didn't call me already."

"Of course, I heard the news. Since you were coming, I decided I could wait. I'll pour you a glass of wine. We can make ourselves comfortable in the living room and you can tell me everything. After that you'll tell me why Vincent didn't come with you."

Ten minutes later, Xavier had filled his mom in on what had happened this morning and was just gearing up for the *why Vincent called things off part* when her phone rang. Saved by the bell. While he'd been talking, the dogs greeted each other. Mop kept twirling in a circle while Berkeley and Lebowski stood and watched her.

"Just a sec, hon, let me get that."

It was Max, of course. Xavier listened to their mom's side of the conversation, more than a little pleased it was his brother she was irritated with and not himself.

"Well," she huffed, setting her phone down on the couch. "I just don't know what to do with that boy."

Mop, tired of trying to get the other dogs to play, huffed and plopped down at Wanda's feet.

"He's not a boy, Mom. We'll be forty-three on our next birthday."

"Hush. You two will always be my boys." She released a gusty sigh. "I should have known this DNA thing would affect him. It's always the quiet ones you should worry about. Now," she said, eyeing him, "where is Vincent?"

Xavier told her what had happened and shared his theory about the dark place where Vincent's brain had gone.

His mom nodded her agreement, reaching over and squeezing his knee.

"You've got this. Vincent just needs a little time to process." She grinned. "Plus, you have Romy on your side. She's not going to let her dad pull a fast one."

"Speaking of fast ones, what's really going on with you and Rufus?"

It was nice seeing his mom smile. And dammit, if it was Rufus Ferguson that put a smile on her face, Xavier was just going to have to suck it up and deal with it.

"We're dating and enjoying life. Rufus is a sweet man, he gets me."

Sweet. Not how he thought of Rufus, but it wasn't Xavier's business.

"So, what are you going to do to get Vincent back? Not that I think you've lost him."

"Give him some space, but not too much."

It took everything Xavier had in him to give Vincent time to think, to come to his senses. But by Wednesday, four full days after their interrupted morning walk, Xavier reached the end of his limited amount of patience. Needing to get out of the house, and force himself to quit checking out his window to see if Vincent was home, he took himself down to the pub. It didn't help his cause—at least Xavier didn't think so—that everybody in town was speculating about Lizzy and what had happened to her.

At the Stop-N-Go. At Pizza-Mart. The Steam Donkey. Probably the ranger station—because Critter's lips flapped like laundry in the wind. Even Sydney Baskin at the appraisal office. Everywhere Xavier turned, the talk was all about Lizzy Harlow. And no doubt at the high school too. Even worse, some residents had coupled the remains found in the woods with Lizzy's death and speculated that Cooper Springs had a serial killer.

Specifically, one resident.

"No," Xavier said, making himself comfortable on the empty bar stool he'd snagged. "we don't have a serial killer."

He hadn't moved back to town, invested everything he had, taken a risk on his not-so-straight-laced neighbor, only to be thwarted by a damn serial killer.

"How do you know?" Nick Waugh asked, his tone belligerent. Xavier already regretted taking the seat next to him.

"Serial killers are actually very rare." Xavier had looked up the stats. "Less than one percent of murders in a year. And nothing connects what happened to Lizzy with the remains Jayden found."

Although Jayden's grim discovery followed two weeks later by his mom's unnatural death was terrible timing. Not that there was a good time for either tragic event.

"That stat doesn't mean we don't have one here," Nick insisted. "It just means we could be the unlucky ones, the one percent."

Nick was obviously a glass-half-empty guy. Or maybe he was the kind of person who assumed there was no reason for anyone to fill his glass.

Magnus plunked Xavier's wine down in front of him and then focused his attention on Nick. "Zip it. The last thing we need around here are rumors of a serial killer."

"Agreed," said Xavier. "Is Corey Harlow back yet?"

Next to him Nick snapped his lips shut and scowled at his beer.

"Last I heard from Forrest, Harlow is supposed to get in today or tomorrow. There was a bit of delay with where he was stationed."

"Do you know him at all?" Xavier asked.

Magnus shook his head. "Not really. In passing, I suppose. He left for college and the next thing I heard he was in the Navy. Somewhere along the way he married Lizzy. I never understood why they lived out in Zenith. People say Cooper Springs is a ghost town, but Zenith is the real thing."

"What about Lizzy, did you know her?"

Here he was mining the rumor mill when he wanted to be breaking down Vincent's front door. He was as bad as anyone else in town.

Another shake of the head. "Didn't know her at all."

"Vincent told me she was friends with his ex-wife. But that must have been a while back."

"Carly Barone," Magnus said, shifting so he was leaning against the bar. "There's someone I was glad to see leave town. How's Vincent doing after"—he twitched his eyebrows—"you know."

"I was there too," Xavier groused.

"Yeah, and here you are, bellying up to the bar on a Wednesday. You're never in here on Wednesdays, you're generally a Thursday through Saturday guy."

Xavier huffed, but Magnus had a point.

"He's a bit freaked out."

Magnus eyed him. "Pushed you away, did he?"

"How do you know?" Had Vincent been talking to Magnus?

An irritating smirk crossed Magnus's lips. Pointing his thumb at his own chest, he said, "Publican. It's what I do."

"Huh."

"Seriously, why are you sitting here giving him time to come up with more reasons to push you away?"

"I'm giving him some space, time."

"He's had enough of both. Drink up and get out of here."

TWENTY-TWO

VINCENT

Vincent

A knock on the front door startled Vincent from glaring at paperwork. He had it spread out across the kitchen table—life insurance policies, the college savings program, bills that needed attention. Things he could control.

"Will you get that?" he called out to his daughter. "I'm in the middle of something." In the middle of doing everything he could to not crawl across the street and apologize to Xavier. Never answering the door unless he knew it wasn't Xavier on the other side was one of those things. "And I'm not home," he added.

He'd made the right decision. It was his job to protect their tiny family, he reminded himself for the thousandth time since Saturday afternoon. Romy was holed up in her bedroom. He'd been on the receiving end of the silent treatment since calling it off with Xavier. Except for the random muttered comments about "Dad acting like a pimply freshman."

From her bedroom Vincent heard an exasperated groan followed by the sound of Romy's footsteps crossing the living room and then the front door opening. She knew he was avoiding Xavier, seeing as he'd been leaving for work before seven all week and parking around the block when he got home at night.

"Is your dad here?"

Xavier's deep voice immediately undermined Vincent's resolve. He actually started to rise from his chair but stopped himself.

No.

He needed more time before seeing Xavier face to face again.

When he'd finally gotten home Saturday, freezing cold and reeling from the day's events, Vincent had immediately told Romy things were over between him and Xavier. There was no point in having her think otherwise. He'd blurted the news out and been met with the kind of disdain that only teenaged girls were capable of.

Her eyes narrowed *and* one eyebrow raised, Romy had shaken her head at him—like *he* was the teenager—and said, "Whatever. But I'm still helping Wanda with Mop and Berkeley."

Was there a word more chilling and dismissive than *whatever*?

He'd started to defend himself—as if *he'd* made the wrong decision—and had to remind himself *he* was the adult, and it was *his* life. Except, of course, that wasn't why he'd called things off.

Ignoring him, Romy had grabbed an apple from the fruit basket and a bottled tea from the fridge and left the kitchen for her room, where she'd stayed except for school, drama club, and walking Wanda's dogs.

From his seat at the table Vincent heard her tell Xavier, "No."

Was it possible for more disdain to be packed into that two-letter word? At least she was honoring his decision and not inviting Xavier inside. Although he felt crappy having his daughter lie for him.

"So, Romy." Xavier's voice made his heart pound against his ribs and uninvited butterflies zoom around his stomach. "I was wondering if you could give me a hand and hang out with

Lebowski for an hour or two. I'll pay you of course. He ate something funny today and I'm—er, *need* to leave the house for a bit."

What had Lebowski eaten? Hopefully not something poisonous, that could be dangerous. Xavier should take him to the vet. Of course, there wasn't a vet in Cooper Springs, so he'd have to go to Aberdeen.

"Sure, let me grab my coat." Her tone was sweeter than honey. "I'm gonna bring my homework, if that's okay? I'll be over in a sec."

"Thanks, I owe you one."

There were rustling noises as Romy grabbed her backpack and, presumably, her coat.

Then she yelled, "I'm going to watch Lebowski for a little while." Which totally negated her lie for him. And as if he hadn't heard the whole exchange.

Vincent didn't bother to reply, he just needed Xavier to not be standing at the front door. Mere feet from where Vincent was eavesdropping. Feet from where Vincent was waiting, wanting, and wishing things could be different.

The door shut and Vincent sucked in a sigh of relief. This was good. He focused on his laptop, trying to remember what he'd been doing before Xavier's knock interrupted everything.

"One thing I know from growing up with a single parent is, it's hard."

Vincent's head shot up—to Xavier, who was leaning against the kitchen door frame.

"Wha—?"

Xavier held up one hand. "Nope, you had your turn, now it's mine." Taking off his out-of-Vincent's-price-range wool coat, Xavier folded it and tossed it behind him, in the direction of the couch.

Then Xavier moved toward Vincent. He felt like prey.

Xavier didn't sit down.

"I know what it's like, from a kid's perspective anyway, to

worry about everything. You're a fixer, Vincent, a caretaker. And the number one person in your life is Romy. Which is as it should be."

Pulling out the chair opposite him, Xavier sat. Vincent opened his mouth again, and once again, Xavier held up his hand.

"Fuck." He paused, scraping his fingers through his thick hair. "I'm no good at this shit, at all. There are no guarantees, right? Lizzy Harlow was alive one day and gone the next. But one thing I do know for sure is that it's impossible to insulate yourself from life. Terrible things happen to good people, a person can do *everything* right in their life and still terrible things happen to them or the people they love. The one thing we *can* do is accept the good things when they come along. For me, Vincent Barone, you are a good thing."

Reaching across the table, Xavier gently pushed the laptop lid closed. His action hardly registered because Vincent found himself too mesmerized by Xavier's eyes. Not by their unusual color—although he always noticed that—but by their expression. They blazed with emotion.

"I know we're just getting to know each other but... we've also known each other a long time. You and I are the same goofy kids we were in high school. You're still trying to make sure nobody gets hurt. I'm still Chaos Boy—thank you for that title, Mom. I like to think I've toned it down a bit. My chaos has a direction these days."

The furnace squeaked and rumbled as it switched on and sent a blast of warm air out of the vent near Vincent's feet.

"Anyway, what I am doing a terrible job of saying is, you can't control the terrible shit, but you can control the good. Let me be part of the good things in your life. Don't push me away because of what might happen. I'm not saying let's run off and get married—but at least give us a chance. I understand Romy comes first for you, but who do you come first for?"

He pointed at his chest. "Me, Vincent. You come first for me."

"Did Lebowski really eat something bad?" Vincent wanted to know.

Xavier stared at him for a minute then laughed. And kept laughing. Tears streamed from his eyes, and, snorting, he lifted a hand and wiped them away.

"I come over here and bare my soul and you want to know about my dog." He snorted again. "Lebowski is just fine."

"Good."

Vincent's poor heart was doing all sorts of weird fluttering and he couldn't tell if it was anxiety or happiness. Maybe it was a little of both. Xavier claimed Vincent came first for him. Had he ever come first for anyone? His parents had loved him, but they'd been older and not quite sure what to do with a child. Carly—no, Carly had come first for Carly.

"I promised myself I'd give you time to think, but we both know I have the patience of a toddler. And to be fair, it's been three and a half days."

Against his better judgment, Xavier's words had Vincent smiling, his heartbeats smoothing out.

"I just, this feels so fast." Vincent waved his hand between them. "Like a car careening out of control, no brakes, a cliff on one side and no shoulder to pull off on."

"So," Xavier said. He smiled and captured Vincent's flailing fingers. "We take it slow. This is you and me. We can do whatever feels right to us."

"You've just admitted you're not patient," Vincent pointed out.

"If we're slow *together*, that's totally different. Look, we don't need to get married, we don't even need move in together. I'm not against either of those things but we don't have to do them right away. Or ever. If that's what you want."

Opening his mouth, Vincent wasn't sure what he'd intended to say, but what came out was, "I'm scared."

Xavier stood up and held his hand out to Vincent. "Me too. Can we be scared together?"

Without thinking, Vincent rose to his feet. Grabbing onto Xavier's hand like it was the only thing keeping him from drowning—maybe it was.

"I'm gonna kiss you now," Xavier warned.

"All talk and no action," Vincent teased, his voice a bit shaky. He could tease now. The lump in his throat that had kept him from taking a deep breath since Saturday afternoon softened. It wasn't gone but it had diminished.

Their lips met. This kiss wasn't a frantic, gnashing demand, it was a promise. Lifting his hands, Vincent cupped Xavier's cheeks. He hadn't shaved, and the rough of his light beard under Vincent's fingertips made his heart pound for entirely different reasons.

He didn't know how long they stood there reveling in each other before Xavier leaned away and looked him in the eye.

"So, scared together? We'll see where this takes us?"

Vincent nodded. "I'm pretty sure I know where we're headed —and trust me, it's good, but I'm not ready *yet*."

Leaning in again, Xavier rested his forehead against Vincent's. "Together, we'll get there *together*."

TWENTY-THREE
EPILOGUE

Xavier– Mid-August

"Showtime in half an hour," Xavier said with excitement. "This is really happening."

"It's not the Minack, but it will do." Hands on his hips, Magnus surveyed the stage and seating area for the Summer Beach Shakespeare production of *The Tempest*.

Xavier was pleased too. Tickets weren't sold out, but a decent crowd of forty or fifty brave souls was expected tomorrow night and through the weekend. Four shows, Friday through Sunday, two evening performances and two matinees. And next year, Xavier hoped they could run the festival over two weekends.

Putting on this production was never going to bring in fistfuls of money but that wasn't what this was about. This was bringing the community together and drawing in visitors who would come back for more. Who would spend their hard-earned dollars in Cooper Springs.

Tonight was the final dress rehearsal.

The weather was perfect, not a cloud in the sky. In fact, the weekend forecast was for clear skies and temperatures in the high seventies. Ticket holders wouldn't freeze or get rained out. And they might not even need a jacket, although everyone was encouraged to bring blankets and wraps for when the sun went down.

Guest seating was a set of bleachers the players borrowed from the high school. It had been tucked up inside a slightly inset section of the mile-long bluff that overlooked the beach. The stage, such as it was, was in front of the seats and each actor would have a wireless mic clipped to them that linked to the sound system Lani and Mags had rigged up.

Was it perfect? Absolutely not. Would it work? Would theatergoers leave with lifelong memories of Magnus bringing back his interpretation of Prospero along with several other of Cooper Springs' amateur actors—Liam Wright, Forrest Cooper, Xavier's mom, Mags, and Critter, just to name a few—making their stage debuts? All Xavier's fingers and a few of his toes were crossed.

"What's the Minack?" asked Vincent, coming to stand next to him.

Xavier eyed his boyfriend, wanting to lick him like he was an ice cream cone. Vincent was a little sweaty from putting the finishing touches on the stage and the set they'd designed—Romy had helped with it too but wasn't able to attend the dress rehearsal. Vincent wore a deliciously tight t-shirt with the sleeves cut off, very much putting his muscles on display.

"It's an outdoor theater in Cornwall. I went there once, years ago," Magnus said. "Beautiful. But enough of that, we've got a show to rehearse." He clapped his hands trying to get the attention of the rest of the cast. Magnus liked to think he was in charge and, with the exception of Forrest, most let him get away with it.

Xavier, Vincent, and a few other volunteers were tonight's test audience. Not that they hadn't already seen the production several dozen times since they started rehearsals a few weeks ago.

"I should run home and change," Vincent said, looking down at the damp shirt clinging to his chest.

"You don't need to change. Just put your sweatshirt on, you're distracting me."

Vincent rewarded Xavier's comment with a very slow up-and-down glance, taking in everything about him.

"You're wearing those shoes," Vincent remarked in a *tone*.

Xavier looked down at his feet. He was in fact wearing the golden Alessandro Galet Scritto leather oxfords Arsen had given him. The things were damn near indestructible. He'd worn them to rainy football games. To a spring soccer tournament. They'd protected his feet several times when he visited Levi Cruz's orchards *and* Forrest's lavender fields.

They continued to look just fine.

Vincent set his toolbox down on the edge of the stage and held his hand out.

"Give me those shoes."

Xavier squinted at him. "Excuse me, what?"

"Give. Me. Those. Damn. Shoes."

Xavier hesitated a second too long. The next thing he knew he was flat on his ass in the sand, his feet up in the air and Vincent was standing over him wrenching the Italian leather off his feet.

"What the fuck are you doing?" He twisted his legs but that only helped Vincent get the shoes off faster.

"I'm getting rid of these things once and for all."

Leaving Xavier lying in the sand, Vincent started toward the ocean, eating up the yards with his long strides. And Xavier's footwear in his hands.

"What the hell?"

Scrambling to stand up—while Magnus brayed like a donkey on acid—Xavier started after Vincent. He had to stop and pull off his socks before starting up again.

"Hold up," he called after Vincent. "Jogging in sand is not as romantic or fun as it looks in the movies!"

Vincent did not hold up. If anything, he started moving faster.

Xavier chased after him, but Vincent was too damn quick. When he finally reached the high tide line, he was able to put on a burst of speed because the sand there was firm instead of moving each time he took a fucking step.

"What the fuck are you doing?" he managed to gasp as he closed in on his boyfriend.

He caught up to Vincent just as he swung his arm backward. Seconds later he hurled one of the shoes as far as he could into the surf. The overpriced loafer soared heel over toe above the crest of a wave, smacking against the surface of the water and then disappearing from view.

"I could've just thrown them away, you know," Xavier panted, bending over as he worked on re-oxygenating his lungs.

"Nope. This is much more satisfying," Vincent replied, winding up his arm like he was a major league baseball player and pitching the other shoe as far into the ocean as he could manage. This time the shoe floated for a few seconds before being swallowed by the deep.

"The tide is just going to bring them back," Xavier pointed out.

"Maybe, but the tide is still going out, so I have hope that they will be carried far out to sea where a sperm whale will eat them."

"That poor whale will probably have indigestion for weeks."

Xavier sucked more air into his tortured lungs—maybe he needed to see if someone was interested in starting a small gym in town. He was definitely out of shape. They could even offer daily and weekly passes to visitors.

"Besides, if I'm going to move in with you," Vincent continued, "I'm not living with those damn shoes."

Xavier breathed in wrong and choked on his own spit. Great,

Vincent was finally agreeing to move in, but Xavier was going to suffocate to death on his saliva.

"You all right?" Vincent asked, pounding him vigorously on the back.

"Fine," he rasped. "Just fine." Waving Vincent off, Xavier straightened again. "You hate those shoes? That's why you wouldn't move in with me?"

"Yes, I hate those shoes. A few months ago, I decided when I hated them enough, I was ready to move in. I'm not living with 'em, so the shoes have to go."

Xavier was stunned and stupidly happy.

"You're really going to move in with me. You and Romy?"

He'd been so careful not to pressure Vincent about moving. He'd promised to be patient but... patience had proven to be even more challenging than he'd expected.

"We're really going to move in with you," Vincent said with a smile. "If the offer is still open. Romy will be graduating in a couple years anyway, and who knows what she'll decide to do, where she'll live."

Romy was insisting she was going to study criminology. Vincent had told Xavier he was conflicted by her career choice, but Xavier knew he would support his daughter no matter what she did. Xavier would too of course; he and Romy had forged their own goofy relationship since last October.

"I want you to move in. I've wanted it for a while." There'd been nights where he'd hated that Vincent was just across the street and not in Xavier's bed. The past ten months had involved a lot of late-night sexting.

Holding Xavier's gaze, Vincent stepped into his space, their chests colliding. Xavier imagined he could feel Vincent's heartbeat. Vincent slid his warm hand around the back of Xavier's neck, holding him in place.

"Thanks for waiting," Vincent murmured before pressing his mouth against Xavier's.

"I would have waited forever," Xavier fudged.

Vincent smiled against his lips. "Liar."

≈

Are you ready for more Reclaimed Hearts? **Below Grade**, Martin and Nick's story, is up next. Preorder Below Grade today!

≈

Curious about the Flag Pole Incident? Click HERE to join my newsletter and read all about it! **Warning NSFW**

≈

Below Grade Blurb

A serious health scare forces Martin Purdy to rethink his life. He quits his job, sells his house, and buys a set of fixer-upper cabins on the coast. There's just one teensy problem. Along with the property comes a very angry man.

Nicholas Waugh had his own scare, bad enough that he slunk back to the crappy town he grew up in. With no home to call his own, he finagles a security gig keeping an eye on a set of vacant cabins. The deal comes with a free one-year lease–and he's not leaving a day sooner. Not even if the new owner gets down on his knees and begs him.

Okay… maybe if he got down on his knees.

Fifteen years of teaching college freshmen and patience is second nature to Martin. But Nick is giving Martin a run for his money. He's one suggestive chainsaw sculpture away from justifiable homicide. If that wasn't enough, when he's not infuriated with Nick, Martin finds himself fighting an inappropriate and ridiculous attraction to the much younger man

Stay up to date on all things Elle related by joining the Highway to Elle. A weekly newsletter with all the Elle news you'll ever need!

A THANK YOU FROM ELLE

If you enjoyed *Adverse Conditions*, I would greatly appreciate if you would let your friends know so they can experience Xavier, Vincent, and the rest of Cooper Springs As with all of my books, I have enabled lending on all platforms in which it is allowed to make it easy to share with a friend. If you leave a review for Adverse Conditions or any of my books, on the site from which you purchased the book, Goodreads, Bookbub, or your own blog, I would love to read it! Email me the link at elle@ellekeaton.com

Keep up-to-date with new releases and sales, *The Highway to Elle* hits your in-box approximately every two weeks, sometimes more sometimes less. I include deals, freebies and new releases as well as a sort of rambling running commentary on what *this* author's life is like. I'd love to have you aboard! I also have a reader group called the Highway to Elle, come say hi!

ABOUT ELLE

I write MM romantic suspense set in the Pacific Northwest with some contemporary romance thrown in the mix. I'm passionate about writing inclusive romance with complex characters and a unique sense of place. Characters start out broken, and maybe they're still banged up by the end, but they find the other half of their hearts and ALWAYS get their happily ever after. In 2017 I hit the publish button for the first time and haven't looked back. Being an author is the best job I've ever had and now I have over thirty books available for you to read or listen to! I love cats and dogs. Star Wars and Star Trek. Pineapple on pizza and have a cribbage habit that my husband encourages.

Connecting with readers is very important to me. If you are so inclined join my newsletter, the Highway to Elle to stay up-to-date with everything Elle-related. I can also be found on Facebook, Instagram and occasionally TikTok.

Romantic Suspense Series by Elle Keaton
Shielded Hearts
Veiled Intentions
West Coast Forensics
Reclaimed Hearts
For more information, or to purchase paperbacks or audio, please visit my direct sales website
https://ellekeaton.myshopify.com/
Thank you for supporting this indie author!

Made in United States
Troutdale, OR
11/28/2023

15101095R00141